# THE RAVEN'S CURSE

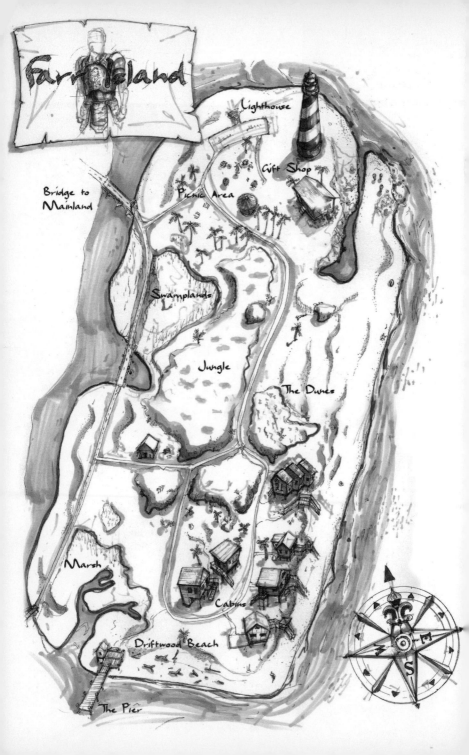

# THE RAVEN'S CURSE

## Lena Wood
✕✕✕✕✕✕✕✕✕✕

Standard
PUBLISHING
Bringing The Word to Life

Text © 2005 Lena Wood.
© 2005 Standard Publishing, Cincinnati, Ohio. A division of Standex
International Corporation. All rights reserved. Printed in U.S.A.
Project editor: Lindsay Black
Content editor: Amy Beveridge
Copy editor: Lynn Lusby Pratt
Cover and interior design: Robert Glover
Cover oil paintings and photography: Lena Wood
Map illustration: Daniel Armstrong
Scripture taken from the HOLY BIBLE, NEW INTERNATIONAL
VERSION®. NIV®. Copyright © 1973, 1978, 1984 by International
Bible Society. Used by permission of Zondervan. All rights reserved. Those
identified *Gullah* are portions of Scripture in *Gullah,* Sea Island Creole.
Copyright © 1995 American Bible Society. Used by permission of the
American Bible Society. All rights reserved.

Library of Congress Cataloging-in-Publication Data

Wood, Lena, 1950-
  The raven's curse / Lena Wood.-- 1st ed.
    p. cm. — (Elijah Creek & the Armor of God ; bk. 3)
  Summary: As Elijah and his friends search for the next piece of armor, the
bond that they have forged sustains them through personal crises and a
terrifying storm.
  ISBN 0-7847-1592-0 (soft cover)
  [1. Christian life--Fiction. 2. Friendship--Fiction. 3. Family problems--
Fiction.] I. Title.
PZ7.W84973Rav 2005
[Fic]—dc22

                                                          2004019562

                          ISBN 0-7847-1592-0

    01  00  09  08  07  06  05          9  8  7  6  5  4  3  2  1

*To the Fam:*
Lusbys, Pratts,
Armstrongs, *and* Summer.
*We stick together.*


*Deepest appreciation to:*
Melanie and Alan Williams
*for hospitality on "Farr Island" and the shrimping lesson*
Zach Hudson *and* Robbie McMath
*for priceless expressions*
Leah Hamilton
*for language assistance*
*&*
The One *who creates blessings out of chaos*

# PART 1: THE RAVEN

*He makes the clouds his chariot*
*and rides on the wings of the wind.*
*He makes winds his messengers,*
*flames of fire his servants.*

—Psalm 104:3, 4

**OKAY,** I'm taking over the story for a while. I'm Skid.

Our search for the whole armor of God had stalled. Sure, things had calmed down—people in town were saying the bodies of Kate Dowland and her baby boy must have fallen in the well by accident all those years ago. A tragedy, nothing more. But when Stan Dowland mysteriously checked out, Magdeline, Ohio, sang another tune. People had suspected the old crackpot of foul play all along, they said, but now it was *really* over. Bruce Theobald's wife would come back to him. The story would fade from the headlines. The souls of the dead Dowlands could all rest in peace. But *we* five couldn't.

Word on the street was that Theobald was still miffed at us guys for exposing his secret love for Kate and his secret hate for Stan Dowland. The police were still holding the belt of truth as possible evidence in the Dowland deaths. And we had no new clues. Then the Wingates went berserk, Robbie shut down, and Elijah shut me out.

Neither Mei nor Reece can tell the story because they

missed out on what happened to us guys that week on the island. To this day Wingate chokes when he talks about it. Someday he might write a musical about the whole screwed up mess and star in it and get famous. But we need an objective eye. So I elect myself.

# Chapter 1

ROBBIE suspected bad times were coming when the biggest raven he'd ever seen took up residence like a weather vane on his raccoon-and-mannequin-infested house—better known as The Castle.

Winter in Ohio was bare and brown—depressing to a kid like me used to the coast and the tropics. We were trudging across Robbie's front yard when this black menace swooped in on the tower and crowed at us: *Wonk! Wonk!*

"Whoa!" I said. "Get a load of that bird!"

Robbie narrowed his big, blue eyes at the bird. It lifted its wings, glided from the rusty roof to a bare tree in the front yard, and tipped its head at us. "Ravens are a sign of bad luck," he said.

I glanced at Elijah, who knew about things in nature. He may not really be Creek Indian like he always hoped, but he's the best I've seen at knowing things about trees and weather and animals: the ways of the wild.

Elijah studied the bird and scanned the sky. "Common raven," he said uneasily. "He's out of his habitat. Ravens stay to mountains and gorges to the north, in New England and Canada." He looked worried about the bird.

Creek's a little strange, but he's all right.

For reasons unknown to us at the time, Elijah Creek

was the heart of our search for the armor of God—ancient battle gear full of secrets and histories we were trying to decipher. The rest of us thought we were along for the ride, that's all. We sat there on The Castle's droopy porch under the raven's beady eye, drinking Mrs. Wingate's hot chocolate with whipped cream and cinnamon sprinkles.

"We're at a standstill," Robbie said, wiping whipped cream off his lip.

"No." Reece bundled against the wind. "This is just down time. Look what we've done in one semester: we found the armor of God buried in Old Pilgrim Church . . ."

"And lost it," Robbie said.

"But found the helmet of salvation near the graveyard," she went on firmly.

"Lost it!" Robbie smirked at Elijah, who had done the losing.

"Ancient history," said Reece, defending Elijah. "We did find it. That's my point."

Mei added, "We know it is somewhere, okay? We found the belt of truth. The rest of the armor is close."

"The belt? Let's see now," Robbie tapped his chin, "where could that be . . . oh yeah, lost that too!" He grinned wickedly, as if he were glad the quest was one step forward and two steps back.

I should've noticed Robbie splintering off from the rest of us at that point. Sure, he could be a whiner; but judging how he could throw himself into long, tiring play rehearsals, tons of library research, and even metal detecting in the dead of winter, my guess was he wasn't really spoiled. Maybe, being an only child, he just liked the attention he got from whining. But something else was going on.

Elijah snapped, "The police have the belt! It's safe and we'll get it back!"

"Yeah, when the case is closed," Robbie sneered, jutting his face out, "which means probably never." He scowled into his cup. "My hot chocolate is cold."

"The police have the Stallards' forensic analysis; Mei made sketches," I said, sounding like a professional relic hunter.

Mei said, "You guys also found the skeletons and solved an old mystery!"

"It's not solved," Robbie argued.

Reece shot him a look and finished, "But almost solved, and all in *one semester!*"

"What is next?" Mei asked. With both hands she sat her cup down on the wicker table. She did everything in a ladylike way: always had a hankie to wipe sweat off her forehead, always kept her hands folded in her lap when she wasn't writing or drawing. While Elijah was grounded over Christmas break, the rest of us had hung out to boost our morale and got to know each other better. Mei told us her name in Japanese letters meant "living sprout." I told her it was true. "You're busting out, moving to your own beat, having your own opinion instead of agreeing with Reece all the time."

Mei liked country music, drawing, swimming, and American movies; and she was a crack tennis player. She was raised with Shinto and Buddhist traditions, but had no belief about the God of the universe. Reece was explaining him to Mei little by little.

Elijah was having a stare-down with the raven. "I say we wait for the belt to be released from the cops. Until then we keep our eyes open."

"The Stallards examined that belt with a fine-tooth comb," Robbie whined. "There's nothing else to learn."

"Have faith, Robbie," Reece said, "a clue will turn up."

She turned to Elijah. "What are we watching for?"

"I don't know yet," he said mysteriously.

I flipped out my Quella, a prototype electronic Bible with concordance, lexicon, and encyclopedia. I punched in *belt of truth* and read the verse out loud: "'Stand firm then, with the belt of truth buckled around your waist, with the breastplate of righteousness in place.'"

"What is breastplate?" Mei asked.

Robbie explained, "It's like a vest but thick and hard."

"The piece of armor that protects the heart, lungs, and liver: the vitals, my dad calls them," I said.

"Vitals? Righteousness?" Mei always kept her electronic Japanese-English dictionary handy, and she started punching in letters.

I peeked over her shoulder. "How do you say *breastplate of righteousness* in Japanese?"

She sucked air through her teeth, a habit we sometimes teased her about: a reverse hiss that meant she didn't know. "It is difficult, I think," she said.

*"Ganbatte,"* I encouraged her.

I go along with the whole idea of learning other cultures. Living all over the world has had its perks, taught me lessons. Mom tells me, "Listen up, Marcus. People in other countries learn English to accommodate us Americans, and we don't usually return the favor. But when *the Skidmores* are in another culture, we *will* know the basics at the very least: how to say good morning and thank you, and how to get around. We will not do or say things that offend others. And always leave a place better than you found it."

Then Dad would say, "It's not that simple, Carlotta. In parts of the world, they'd sooner kill an American as see 'em. Give 'em a gun and they'll prove it. But have a cup of coffee with a guy and he'll tell you he'd like to open a business in America 'cause his kids are starving to death. Now what do you do with that?"

Mom would say, "Uh-huh. I hear you, baby."

Dad always asks questions that nobody can answer.

My point is this: being global puts a whole spin on who I am. Yeah, I'm open to new words and new ways.

Mei found the word and showed us the *kanji* letters, which were cool. "I think it would be *sei gi no mune ate,"* she said, "righteousness of chest shield."

We made her say it several times so we could get it: "Say-ghee-no . . . moo-nay . . . ah-tay."

We tried. She giggled. "You speak good Japanese."

We were pathetic, but it gave Mei a thrill when we took a stab at her language. None of us had bragging rights; she had a hundred English words to every one of our Japanese ones. Reece was ahead of the pack, saying whole sentences in *nihongo,* which is Japanese for "Japanese."

I polished off my hot chocolate. "What do we need to keep going on the armor?"

"Clues," Robbie said sarcastically.

"Oh, you're sharp, Robbie," Reece poked his arm and shivered in her coat, "sharp as the *edge of town!* I have to go inside. I'm freezing." Elijah helped her up. She turned to us. "I know what we need. We need to get into Dowland's house."

Our eyebrows went up. Mei gasped. We'd talked about it before, but it kept getting pushed to the back burner because of the string of bad memories: Salem attacked Elijah in the garage; Dowland had answered Reece and Elijah's visit with screams about hellfire and brimstone; then the old ex-preacher died suddenly, alone in that house.

Reece would have gone back in a heartbeat; the rest of us stood there like dolts.

"Well, we do!" she insisted. "He may have a map of where he hid all the pieces. Or maybe they're in the house, buried in the basement like in the old church. There may be clues the police overlooked. They're looking for a murderer. We're looking for armor."

Robbie finally perked up. "What if he didn't have time to bury the rest, and they're sitting in his closet!" He slapped his forehead. "No more digging. Just go in and get it. Would that be a piece of cake or what?!"

We stepped inside. I yanked the old door closed to keep out as much of the cold as possible. The Castle was so drafty, you could hardly tell a difference between outside and in. Robbie led us down the entry hall to the sitting room where a fire was going.

Standing by the fireplace to warm her hands, Reece broke into an impish grin. "Hey, Elijah, you busted into Dowland's once. Shouldn't be too hard a second time. Your possible jail time would save the rest of us *so* much work. I'd even come visit you."

"The door was *wide open,* and I just went in the garage!" He huffed, went to the window, and looked at the sky. "Sometimes you're a real pain, Reece."

"How would we get in?" Robbie asked.

"Legally," Reece answered, giving Elijah the eye.

Elliston's an edgy girl—defending Elijah one minute, pulling his string the next. And he had a thing for her. So why he bit her head off over a joke, I wasn't sure. Seemed like Robbie's snippy mood was contagious.

Yeah, I should have seen it coming.

# Chapter 2

ON the surface it was life as usual in Magdeline, but the gossip grapevine was going full tilt. I'd taken it upon myself to be the ears of our group around town, so I kept up on it by grabbing breakfast now and then at Florence's restaurant. Anyone who thinks women are the big gossips has never listened in on the old boys' network on a Saturday morning over Florence's rotgut coffee:

"Dowland didn't take the overdose by accident; it was suicide."

"I say it was murder. He was too mean to kill himself."

"Could be Theobald—the old grudge coming to a head."

"Could be someone else. Dowland had enemies, lots of them."

"Could be a random attack. D'ja ever think of that?"

"You mean some psycho on the loose?"

Some days after the raven made his appearance, I skateboarded over to Elijah's. It was a cold and sunny Saturday morning in early February. I was full of coffee and grits. The case was at a standstill. The police wouldn't let us in Dowland's house until they had wrapped things up. They didn't want us messing with the personal effects until they found a next of kin. So far no one wanted to admit being blood relations with the old ex-preacher.

I knocked on the door to Elijah's log house. His mom opened it and said he was in the north section of Camp Mudjokivi—Owl Woods—where he spent a lot of time. He'd used all his Christmas money plus his savings to buy himself a new bow and arrow. The other one seemed fine to me, especially since he'd saved our hides with it, but he was bent on having an upgrade.

Thinking of Elijah's cool bow made me realize something: I needed a weapon of my own, a means of defense to be good at. Since the Salem incident, I was still skittish around dogs, any kind, though I didn't show it. I have a reputation for keeping my cool, and it would be bad form for me to freak out over a toy poodle or something. The problem needed fixing. I figured just having a weapon, even if I didn't use it, might help. My dad's a military man and knows bombs and missiles, but those aren't handy against mad dogs and things like that. I wanted something useful in the wild—like Elijah had—in case he and I were ever shoulder-to-shoulder against another deadly enemy. I was learning a lot by hanging around him.

I spotted Elijah at a distance, shooting arrows up at the high limbs of Great Oak. Elijah didn't turn around, but he knew it was me, probably from the sound of my board zipping through Owl Woods. He kept his arm flexed steady-as-steel across his outstretched bow, aimed at the treetop.

I ditched my skateboard. "Hey."

"Hey."

I stood quiet while he aimed and shot a beanbag hanging from a swaying limb, dead on.

"Big game?"

"Yeah."

"That going to be your dinner?"

He laughed a little. "Yeah."

He ignored me for a while, shooting at another bag and missing twice. Something was wrong.

After a while when he looked back to see if I was still there, I asked, "What's up?"

He turned back, pulled another arrow from his quiver, and aimed. "Nothing."

I waited a minute.

"Nothing," he said again.

I knew it was something. "Honest Injun?"

He shot me a look. I smirked. I don't usually make Indian jokes around Elijah, but I wanted a rise out of him. He smirked back. He knew I was kidding because if anyone knew about ethnic insults, it was me. I'd been called everything from half-breed to hybrid to scary freak. Once a man in a store yelled at me, "How'd a blankety-blank like you get those blankety-green eyes?" I was little then, and I ran home crying to dad. He shoved me in front of a mirror and made Mom come stand there with us. "Son, you look the way you do because your parents are Dom and Carlotta.

Live with it." I was cured of reacting to ethnic slurs after that. Someone calls me a freak now, I just think to myself, *You're the son of Dom and Carlotta. Live with it, man.*

If I could have gotten Elijah to start talking, he'd have run on and on. But today for some reason, he wasn't into it.

"You want to do something?" I asked. "Shoot some ball?"

He shook his head. "Nah." He shot again and hit the bag dead on, then glanced at me again. There was a scared, angry look in his eyes.

"Okay then," I said, turning my board back toward the camp. "See you around."

"See you."

On Monday, I walked up behind him as he was opening his locker, and I slapped it shut, almost catching his hand. He spun. Elijah was as tall as me, but he was no threat. He was strong and fast, but there wasn't much fight in him.

"You picking a fight?" he asked.

"What if I am?" I snarled.

He just stared at me.

I made a fist and put it to his chin. "I'd punch your lights out just for the fun of it, but you'd tell, you little weasel, and Mom would make me do chores, like dusting the furniture. She'd probably make me wear an apron." I paused for him to get the picture. "I look great in an apron, by the way."

He grinned finally, shoved my fist away, opened his locker, and got his books. We split up. Heading for first lunch, I turned and yelled, "Whatever's good, I'm eating it all. You'll end up in second lunch with the coleslaw of death."

"Fine."

For Elijah not to make a food joke, something was really wrong. When I passed Robbie in the hall, he was in even worse shape. His hair, which had grown out a little over the winter, was sticking out like he hadn't brushed it. His face drooped, he slouched, and dragged his feet. I met him head-on.

There *was* a threat in his face. Robbie, the short and brainy one of our alliance, hissed, "Get out of my way."

He was daring me, almost like he was hoping I'd pop him.

"Whoa!" I backed up. "Lighten up. What's with you?"

He skulked off.

I shrugged it off with a huff, maintaining my cool in case anyone in the hall crowd overheard. Whatever had infected Robbie and Elijah, I wasn't going to let it spread to me. Miranda Varner walked past, flashed a smile at me, and I lost my train of thought about my squirrely friends until later.

"What's wrong?" Mom asked when I sauntered into our condo after school. She anticipated my answer. "And don't say 'nothing.' You're not looking at an idiot here. Moms know."

"My friends hate my guts and I don't know why," I said.

"Did you lie to them?" She planted a kiss on my face as I passed and patted me with her red polished fingers.

"No."

"Did you cheat? steal? insult?" She had a grocery list of sins.

"No, no, and no. I'm a saint."

She laughed. "I see. Maybe they're turned off by your need to be worshiped."

I stuck my head in the refrigerator and shrugged. "Search me."

"We're having enchiladas tonight. If you need something, eat fruit." She poured stuff in a bowl and stirred it. "Are the boys generally moody?"

"Robbie can be, I guess. But Elijah . . ." I shoved the fridge door shut and grabbed an apple out of a bowl on the counter.

"Even-tempered?" Mom suggested.

"I guess."

"They're cousins, right?"

"Yeah."

Mom stirred ingredients in the bowl and thought awhile. "It will come out, whatever it is, hon. Hang tight, you hear. Homework?"

"No."

"How many enchiladas do you want?"

"Twenty-eight."

She laughed. "And what for lunch tomorrow?"

Though I joked with Elijah about the school food, Mom usually fixed my lunch. American school lunches are unbalanced, she said. "Pizza and corn, pizza and cake, pizza and pizza. It's outrageous." She likes to cook strange food from the places we've been, so I never know what's for lunch. But it's always good, and everyone wants some. Once I told her she should drive by school as the buses unload and sell lunches out of the trunk, but she waved me off and said, *"Pshh!"*

"Lunch?" I thought out loud. "Hmm . . . surprise me."

# Chapter 3

MOM said to hang tight, but I didn't want to hang tight. I wanted to know. The next morning at school, I came up behind Elijah's back and slammed his locker again. He dropped his head and kind of smiled.

"Take this outside?" I threatened.

He blew out air in a long sigh. "You need to ask Robbie."

I leaned in and said secretly, "I'm afraid of Robbie."

He snorted. He got his books and glanced around. "It's too crowded to talk here."

"I need to ask you about weapons sometime too. I need a weapon," I said. We headed for class.

He said, "Robbie's got you scared, huh?"

"Terrified. I'm on heavy meds for my nerves."

I might have known Elijah wouldn't tell me, but he'd already told Reece. They were always crowding each other into corners at school about one secret thing or another. She met me in the hall with a look of concern on her face and said, "If you haven't noticed. . . ."

"I have."

She sighed. "You'll have to ask Robbie."

"I know the procedure," I said.

"Say a prayer. It's bad," she said softly and walked off

using her cane. I was still in the dark. I wasn't going to ask Robbie. He'd slug me for sure, even knowing I could take him out. I didn't want to go there.

I showed up uninvited at Elijah's house after school. "You got time to talk weapons? I want to protect myself from killer dogs, things like that."

"I have a tomahawk," he said, "but the blade's dull. You could sharpen it up and try it out. It chops trees, little ones anyway. Or my dad has hunting knives."

We flipped through one of Elijah's Indian books.

"I haven't asked Robbie yet," I pried.

"I'm not supposed to talk about it."

So it was a *family* secret.

"Is he sick?"

"No."

"He's moving away," I prodded.

Elijah paused again as if he didn't know. I backed off, getting a hunch. I changed the subject. "Hey, anything on the Dowland case?"

He shook his head. "'Piece by piece . . .'" He was quoting the riddle entwined with the mystery of the armor, what Dowland had said as he sank into madness. Since at first the whole armor had been buried in a scary old church, and since the belt of truth had led us to Kate Dowland's bones, Elijah and I had begun to wonder if every piece of the armor had a grisly past.

"Hey, check this out," I suggested, "if the belt of *truth* uncovered the town's *lies,* do you think the breastplate of *righteousness* just might unearth something . . . *un*righteous?"

He looked up from his book. "You mean evil?"

"Yeah."

"Dad told me the police are going through Dowland's papers, looking for clues about other suspicious deaths."

"To find out if he's buried any other people around town?" I asked.

"Yeah, people who supposedly left him and Old Pilgrim Church but maybe never left town at all."

We thought on that awhile, flipping through books. "Let's get something to eat," he said and took off downstairs. "So you think the breastplate of righteousness is buried in the most evil place in town?"

"Maybe," I followed him. "Where would that be?"

"How should I know?" he said.

"You've lived here longer, Creek. Haven't you sniffed out all the evil places yet?" I smirked.

We raided his refrigerator, dumped sandwich makings on the counter, and got to work building our food.

"How about the pool hall?" he suggested.

"It's a dump but not evil. How about other hole-in-the-wall places, like that palm reader's cottage, The Crystal See?"

"I never paid attention. I'm too busy with camp. Anyway, palm reading's not evil," he said, but it was more of a question.

"It's lying and cheating, trying to contact the dead. Not the party game it's cracked up to be."

He gave me a look.

"I know what I'm talking about. There's voodoo in my background."

"Well, that stuff's not real," he said with a curious expression.

"Maybe, maybe not. Getting caught at sorcery used to carry a death sentence in the old time. In case you didn't know, the spirit world is not a safe place."

For a minute he seemed restless, worried. We took our sandwiches back to his room.

"How about Lowe's Bar on the edge of town?" he suggested.

I shook my head. "More sad than bad. I'm talking a place that Dowland would think was pure evil."

"The bank that closed down his church? Or a lawyer's office," he suggested.

I laughed. "Hey, how about Mr. Kornblume's house?" Kornblume was the biology teacher, an alcoholic whose aquarium fish had a habit of going belly-up. Kids thought he stashed his booze in the tank. "That's pretty evil . . . pickling poor little fishies."

We looked out over his backyard to the lodge and the pool. "What about Telanoo?" I asked.

Elijah shook his head. "I've been over it. No new holes dug."

"You've swept the whole thing?" I said doubtfully.

"There've got to be hundreds of acres back there."

"There are, but I've been over it. More than once."

"Do you *live* out there?" I pictured him after school and on weekends, in the snow and wind and icy rain, all alone. The Brill brothers always gave him grief about working at a year-round camp, calling him Nature Boy. Sometimes I joined in. But I was seriously impressed with his wilderness skills. "You're radical."

He grinned a little.

"Ever get scared back there?"

"I keep moving," he said quietly.

"It's a wonder you're not antisocial, Creek. I guess if Dowland ever followed you back there, he probably caught on that you knew the wilderness like the back of your hand." I paused. "How about Mitch Bigelow's house? He deals drugs."

"Dowland wouldn't know that. Mitch deals to high schoolers." He got the tomahawk off the top shelf of his closet. "Try this out. Let's go sharpen it; Dad has a whetstone in the maintenance building."

We headed across Camp Mudj, still thinking of evil places in town.

"School cafeteria," Elijah suggested with a deadpan face.

"I think you nailed it," I laughed. "Don't be surprised if you find a giant piece of armor in your creamed corn tomorrow."

# Chapter 4

※※※※※※※※※※※※※※※※※※※※※※※※※※※※※※※※※※※※※※※※※※※※

**WHILE** Elijah and I were talking weapons, Robbie had stashed himself in the public library, researching Magdelinians who had died or left town mysteriously. We tracked him down to a dark corner, hunched over stacks of newspapers.

"Hey, Frankenstein, why are you hiding?" I joked. He looked up. He couldn't smile, couldn't even fake one. "Anything new on Dowland?" I asked.

"He had no other children that I can find. It must be his wife buried in that unmarked grave, since he was the only one around the church after it closed. Old Obie told us she died, but not when or how. I can't find anything about it."

"The Romeos said she left town. Should we dig?" I asked.

Robbie's eyes went wide. "No! No digging!"

Elijah said, "From now on the police do the grave-digging. We got into big trouble before."

While Elijah sat across from Robbie and watched him work, I wandered through the travel section to the history aisle. I was riffling through a book on medieval weapons when I overheard a couple of women in the next aisle peeking at Robbie and muttering something about the Wingates. I kept flipping pages and perked my ears.

I headed home for dinner, but not before zipping past The Castle. There was a For Sale sign stuck in the front yard. Finally, the pieces fell into place. Robbie's parents were splitting up. I knew the telltale signs because it had happened to me. I stood there staring at the sign, feeling bad, like getting thumped in the chest with a fist.

Mom was sitting at the counter in the kitchen, chatting on the phone. I plopped down across from her. She saw the look on my face and finished up.

"What is it, baby?"

"They're splitting up. Robbie's parents."

My mom's a gutsy person, but her eyes filled with tears. She came around and hugged me a long time. "We'll have to be there for them, won't we?"

I felt five years old. "He's heading into the horrible time."

"Yes, they all are. So you be strong for Robbie. Be kind."

"I will. I'm a saint, Mom," I joked.

"Yes, you are, Marcus. I know you are."

I was waiting for Elijah at his locker the next day.

"Figured it out," I said.

"You want the tomahawk?" he asked. "No prob."

"No, you dud. I mean Robbie. His parents split."

He riffled through his locker. "Yeah."

"Why?"

"I don't know." He slammed the locker door shut and snorted. "Uncle Dorian met . . . somebody else."

"What Robbie's going through . . . I've been there,"
I said after a while. He gave me a confused look. "They
split up and got back together. It was a few years ago," I
explained. "We've got to be strong for Robbie."

He said, "Yeah," but he didn't have a clue. His mom and
dad are tight; there was no way he got it.

I told Elijah he should call a powwow without Robbie.
He didn't like the idea, but Reece could see my point. "I'll
invite Mei over to my home after school. You two just show
up whenever. Bring your map, Elijah," said Reece. "We can
do some armor business while we're at it."

Robbie didn't come to school the rest of the week. He was
sick. Bad for him, but good for us. None of us liked the feeling
of conspiring against him, having a Robbieless powwow.

Reece and her mom lived in a little apartment they
made up like a dollhouse with lace and light colors. They're
both small and blond and have little bird voices, and they
hug people a lot. But it's a trick, that's what I think—a
camouflage. The Elliston women are tough as nails
underneath. Reece treats her bone condition like it's no big
deal, though who knows what her future will be. There's no
man in the house to fix things or help with the bills. Her
dad lives far away, and her mom works two jobs and does
all kinds of teaching and volunteering at church. Reece says
her mom hardly sleeps.

We sat around the white kitchen table. Reece's mom had
made snacks ahead of time: little sandwiches and brownies.

I said, "Okay, what about Robbie?"

"I'm going to talk to him," Reece said.

Elijah said, "He doesn't want to talk about it."

"I know it's embarrassing, but we can't just ignore it," she answered. "I was little when mine happened, and I don't remember much except feeing afraid and ashamed. Skid's been through it."

"Horrible time," I said. "Horrible."

Reece's mom came in and we fell quiet. She dropped her stuff on the couch.

Reece said, "Hi, Mom. We're talking about Robbie."

Mrs. Elliston went around the table and hugged our heads. "How you kids holding up?"

"We're good," Elijah answered.

"Good, thank you," said Mei.

I nodded. Reece's mom made herself some tea in a fancy little cup and scooted up a chair. "I stopped by the police station," she said. "The autopsy on Mr. Dowland did in fact show an overdose. Whether accidental death or suicide is still being disputed because . . ." She took a sip. "Officer Taylor said there *were* signs of a struggle."

Elijah perked up. "Signs?"

"Of a struggle," she repeated. "They don't know if Dowland went into an insane tirade before he killed himself, whether he lost his mind and took an accidental overdose and fought it at the end, or if someone came in and there was a fight."

"Theobald," said Elijah.

"Revenge," I added.

"And there's some new evidence they're not talking about. Officer Taylor has confided in me because you kids are involved; he's concerned about you." She smiled.

"New evidence?" Elijah asked.

"They're not talking," Reece's mom said.

"So," Reece said, "it's possible that Theobald did kill Kate Dowland and her child all those years ago. When the story came out, he went over to Mr. Dowland's to shut him up?"

"Don't spread that around," Mrs. Elliston warned.

Elijah said, "He already told the police I lied."

She sized up Elijah. "Old footprints aren't so easy to track. Final word from the police department through me: steer clear of Theobald and anything relating to the case. Officer Taylor knows what snoops you kids are." She slapped the table and smiled. "Anyone want seconds?"

When we finished eating, I nodded Elijah over to the window while the girls were busy talking to Reece's mom. The second floor window had a sweet view of the woods and hills beyond. "Nice view," I said as he came beside me.

"Yeah."

"The most evil spot in town," I hinted, "in Dowland's mind could be . . . "

"Theobald's." He was following my line of thought.

"We have to check it out, look for a fresh dig."

# Chapter 5

ON Monday, Reece and Mei were waiting at Elijah's locker. Reece was fuming. "How are you guys expecting to spy out Theobald's place without getting caught, or shot?"

I threw Elijah a look. Obviously he had leaked that piece of information to his ladylove, but was trying to play innocent. I tipped my head calmly to Reece. "We'll use stealth."

"You're not using anything," she snipped.

"It's our only lead," I said.

"Not a chance," she persisted.

*"Abunai,"* Mei said. "Dangerous."

"You have a brilliant plan?" I asked Reece.

She thought a moment. "Give me a week. The ground's half frozen anyway. You couldn't dig."

Elijah slung his backpack over his shoulder. "We wait so that you can do . . . what?"

She glanced upward. "So I can contact Command Central for further instructions." She winked at me. It was military lingo for prayer.

"Gotcha," I said.

Mom and Dad whispered about the Wingates late at night over coffee. I caught enough to know they were cooking up a plan to help.

Wingate seemed to get shorter and paler every day. He had dark circles under his eyes, and his clothes hung limp; he wasn't eating. But he kept up the research on the lost citizens of Magdeline. Any library information he found about long-gone church members, he turned over to the police. They must have been impressed.

On Monday—a week to the day after Reece started praying—Officer Taylor called with the news that we could have the belt of truth back. Elijah picked it up that afternoon, and we gathered at Robbie's for a fresh look. The raven was still showing up around The Castle, drawing Elijah's attention and keeping us all a little spooked. And Robbie suddenly didn't feel like getting out much. I wasn't sure, but guessed that his dad had moved out. We were going nuts trying to keep it light while his world was crashing down. If I hadn't been through the horrible time myself, I'd have thrashed him over his stinky attitude. But people who tell you to buck up at a time like that are full of hot air.

Since the attic was the most private place, I suggested we mount the belt on a gun rack above the door.

"Hidden in plain sight, like the truth," Reece said slyly.

Elijah wanted to try on the belt first. Robbie blurted out: "Don't do it! It's a bad omen. This whole quest has been nothing but trouble! And ravens are bad luck!"

"Not according to Indian legends," Elijah spoke in a kind voice, like a teacher after you've given the wrong answer. He hooked the buckle into its clasp.

"In the Bible ravens are sometimes good," Reece added.

"Bad news," Robbie insisted. "It landed on my house, not on yours, and look what's happening."

"But remember that *omen* means 'truth,'" I said.

"And that's what I'm saying," he said hysterically. "The bad omen came true!"

Robbie was like a downpour at a picnic.

"There'll be no reasoning with him for a while," Mom warned me when I complained over dinner. "Remember how you acted when Dad left?"

I nodded. "I quit eating."

"You snapped at everyone. You pierced your ear and wore an earring with a dragon on it. You stole money from me." She laughed. "You tore up things and you—"

I put up a hand to stop her. "Okay, okay."

"Just let him vent," was Mom's advice.

"He's a ticking time bomb," I argued.

"And when he goes off, someone needs to be there."

I wasn't excited about getting hit with Robbie's shrapnel. She reached across the table and squeezed my hand. "It brings up the bad stuff. I know. It's okay."

We finished up dinner and cleared off the table. When I wasn't looking, she grabbed me in a bear grip.

*"Tranquilo, me hijo.* Dad's working on a plan."

"A plan?" I said grudgingly, trapped in her hug.

"You'll like it."

"Yeah?"

She whispered in my ear, "Low Country."

I broke loose and spun to face her. "The beach!!??"

"Nothing solid yet."

"When?" I grinned ear to ear.

Mom's eyes sparkled. "Spring break. You three boys."

I punched the air, a victory punch. "Yes!"

I had no idea how it played into helping Robbie, but a week with my dad at the beach house was seriously awesome.

"Not a word until we're sure."

I gave *her* the bear hug this time.


Spring was in the air, as they say, and one warm and windy March afternoon, the five of us decided to go back to where the first piece of the armor had been dug up: beside the lonely grave outside Old Pilgrim Church cemetery. To get there we had to pass the charred hole in the ground where the church once stood. The five of us were drawn to it like moths to a flame.

We stood in a line at the rim of the old basement wall and peered in. Pieces of roof timbers and wooden church pews half filled the blackened hole, like giant sticks of charcoal poking up out of muddy water and ready to collapse. It stunk of wet ashes. The timbers creaked with every gust.

Reece said reverently, "This is where it all began, remember?"

"For you guys. I wasn't here," I reminded her. "It was just you four at the start."

Elijah pointed down to the pile of charred timber. "Under there we found the body-shaped mound. The whole armor of God was buried there at first." He paused. "It could have been so easy . . . if we'd known."

We stared at the hole.

"How could we know?" said Robbie with the faintest hint of concern. "We found it by accident."

Reece shook her head. "It was no accident. It was meant to be. We have to keep looking."

Elijah's eyes were fixed mysteriously on the hole. "Maybe the next piece is right under our noses. . . ." He glanced at the sky distractedly. "If Dowland really wanted to be rid of it, why not bury it back in the basement and set fire to the building?" Suddenly he got excited. "Maybe the city hasn't bulldozed it yet because . . . you know . . ."

"What?" Reece asked.

"Because we're *supposed* to find the next piece, and it's here!"

"Or maybe," I said, being practical, "with Christmas and New Year's and the ground being frozen, they just haven't gotten to it."

Robbie turned away. "Let's go see the reject grave again. Maybe we'll find a clue or something."

"Sure," I said. "We have to start somewhere." Halfway across the cemetery we noticed Elijah wasn't with us. We turned around. He was gone.

# Chapter 6

REECE spun around toward the church. "Elijah?"

Robbie and I took off. Mei stayed back to help Reece.

"You are crazy, man!" I yelled into the hole.

"I can't let them bury it," he called up, his voice strong. "I have to see if it's here. One look, that's all."

"Don't go under those timbers," Reece warned.

"I have to. It's okay. They've been sitting here all winter."

"They're creaking!"

"They're not going anywhere."

He moved like liquid between the rickety timbers, looking back at us once before disappearing into the dark cavern that had once been a crawl space.

"I think he can do it," I said calmly.

Moments passed. "Elijah?" Reece called softly.

No response. But no crumbling and crashing either.

"He's okay," I said hopefully. "It's dark in there. His eyes have to adjust. And he probably doesn't want to make noise, start an avalanche." We waited.

"Come . . . out!" Reece said through gritted teeth.

Above our heads, a *whoosh* . . . the raven sailed in for a landing on the jagged tip of a charred beam.

"Oh no!" yelled Robbie. "The raven's here! Get out, Elijah! You'll be *buried alive!*"

Mei's jaw dropped. She said something in Japanese and put her hands over her face.

Elijah edged out into the light, squinting. He and the raven locked eyes. We stared at them; no one moved. Elijah eased farther out of the hole. A gust of wind startled the bird. Launching itself off the beam, its weight was enough to start the beam sliding. It hit the collapsed roof, bounced off, hit another beam, and sent that one toppling. The roof shuddered.

"Get out!" we screamed.

Elijah shot through the falling timbers, elbowing and ducking and leaping, heading straight for me. I dropped to my belly and reached down for him. He leaped, we grabbed wrists. The tangle of jagged beams tottered in our direction, poised to catch Elijah square in the back.

"Let's go, let's go!" I yanked with all my might.

Then Reece was beside me, her arms reaching out to break the beams' fall.

Elijah scrambled up the wall. I grabbed his jacket, rolled on my back and jettisoned him over my head. And right into Reece. She was thrown to the ground with a thud.

Then the beam crashed, splintering against the basement wall.

I sprang up to see if Reece was hurt. She was flat on her back, stiff as a board. "Reece! Hey, you okay?"

Terror welled up in her eyes. Her mouth was open, but she wasn't breathing.

*We've snapped her like a twig!* I thought.

"Reece!" Elijah dropped to one knee beside me. For a second the same look of terror washed over him. Then he went into camp counselor mode. "Don't panic, Reece. You have the wind knocked out of you. Just relax. Take it easy. Breathe a little, then a little more."

We gathered around her. Elijah and Mei held her hands. A little at a time, she started breathing again.

We forgot about the reject grave and helped Reece to the lodge.

Elijah peeled off his muddy shoes and socks and tossed them in a grocery bag he found in the lodge kitchen. "Don't ever do that again, Reece," he said, coming back to the couch where she sat. "Don't ever try to rescue me."

"You rescued me before," she defended.

"Yeah, but this was different. I was going to make it."

"Actually you weren't, Creek," I said. "If you hadn't cleared the wall the second you did, that beam would have impaled you. Reece was stepping in to break its fall."

"It was the raven's fault," Robbie said flatly. "He wants to kill us because of that omen belt. I say we get rid of it!"

We ignored him.

Reece was back to business in a minute. "Nothing was down there? No armor?"

"No. The crawl space was as empty as before."

"Oh, good!" said Robbie sarcastically. "Terrific."

First thing next day, I caught Elijah at his locker; Robbie

was with him. I laid out the plan for spring break. "We have a beach house, but don't get your hopes up," I said.

"What do you mean?" Robbie asked.

"It's a shack," I admitted.

"On the beach?" Elijah's face lit up.

"What beach?" Robbie asked.

"Farr Island," I said. "You probably never heard of it. Near Hilton Head. Right on the Atlantic Ocean."

"Hilton Head?!" Elijah beamed.

"*Near* Hilton Head," I warned again. "But it's a shack. No pool or tennis courts. Just sand and salt water."

Elijah didn't care. He flipped out, in his own woodsy quiet way, smiling and looking at the floor like he couldn't believe his ears. He took a deep breath.

Robbie's eyes shifted. He couldn't decide how to act over it. "I don't know. . . ."

"Come on. It will be great!" Elijah said, prodding his cousin with everything he could think of: "Surf and sand, babes in swimsuits, no hassles, fun in the sun!"

"It's snowing outside," Robbie grumbled, his face sleepy and hopeless looking.

"That's March in Ohio for you: snowing today, sunny and seventy tomorrow." I nudged him. "Anyhow, break is three weeks away, and we'll be heading south, Bahama Mama. South!!" I did a little jiggy dance.

# PART 2: THE WAVE

*Even the wind and the waves obey him!*

—Mark 4:41

# Chapter 7

WE picked up Robbie and Elijah as the sun burst over the horizon. The moment we zipped past the Magdeline city limits sign, Dad said, "Okay, men. It takes around twelve hours to get to the island. We'll stop for meals at 1200 hours and 1700 hours and pit stops wherever."

While Robbie pouted, stared out the window, and slept, I told Elijah about when we lived near the coast. "Dad's part Gullah," I said.

"I never heard of Gullah," said Elijah.

Dad explained: "It's the name given to east coast tidewater ex-slaves. After the Civil War, whole communities were left to themselves for a long time. They clung to their African heritage and the social ideas of the English, making their own culture. Marcus's grandparents are mixed, white and Gullah. You'll hear some of our folklore this week." He grinned.

"Gullah . . . what's that mean?" Robbie asked sleepily.

"No one's sure," he answered. "Best guess—it comes from the Gola people of West Africa. A lot of slaves were kidnapped from there."

"Gullah have their own language too. Tell 'em, Dad."

Dad kept driving.

Robbie sat up and asked, "You speak another language?" Wingate was always learning.

"It's based on English, sort of like a dialect, but an actual language. Ever heard of gumbo? yams? Those are Gullah words." Dad thought a minute. "Okay, here goes. I'm a little rusty, but I'll tell you a story from the Bible: the resurrection." He cleared his throat. "Real aaly een da maanin de fus day ob de week, befo day clean—" he paused to explain. "*Day clean* is Gullah for 'sunrise.' And I should explain that Jesus has been dead three days already when this part of the story takes up." He continued. "De ooman dem take de spice wa dey done beena mix op an gone ta Jedus tomb. Wen dey git ta de tomb, dey see dat de stone wa done beena kiba de door ta de tomb done been roll baak. So dey gone eenside, bot dey ain't find de Lawd Jedus body. Dey da wonda bout wa done happen, wen all ob a sudden, dey see two man come stan op by um. Dem man habe on bright clothes wa da shine. De ooman been real scaid, an dey bow dey hed down ta de groun. Bot de man dem tell um say, 'Oona aint oughta look yah mongst de ded people fa a man wa da libe, ainty? Jedus ain't yah. E done git op from mongst de ded, an e da libe gin!'"

The guys cracked up.

Dad chuckled. "There you have it: de gospel in de Gullah tongue. Okay, enough of that. You men like shrimping?"

Elijah said he'd like to learn.

"How 'bout you, Wingate?" Dad asked.

"That's fine," he said, half asleep already.

"Men should kill their own food once in a lifetime," Dad said. "Puts things in perspective."

Dad woke Robbie when we crossed the peaks of the Blue Ridge: "Mountains, Wingate. Get an eyeful while you can. We're heading into Low Country." Then he added in a voice dark with mystery, "We gonna get down to de Get Down!" Then he laughed, a rumble deep in his chest.

Elijah and Robbie swapped worried looks. It sounded to me like Dad was up to something.

Toward dinner, we stopped at a truck stop and had steak and eggs. The meal laid heavy; and as the sun sank low in the sky behind us, we guys drifted off one by one.

A while later Dad's rumbling voice woke us up: "We've crossed over, men." We sat up and blinked. Our headlights beamed through a wicked-looking jungle. It felt like home.

"Where *are* we?" Robbie sounded scared.

"Close," Dad said, smiling in the dark, "getting down to the Get Down."

Dad pulled in behind our beach house, an old cottage perched on poles above sand dunes and beach grass, with steps up to a front deck. He cut the engine and opened the car door to the dark, lonely night. "Hear that?"

Sounds of civilization were gone, but a surging whisper came from beyond the dunes.

"The ocean," Elijah said. He bolted from the car and took off, yanking his shoes off as he ran. He didn't say so, but I could tell that being in the car for twelve hours had just about killed him. When the rest of us crossed over the dunes, he was already back, wet to the knees.

Dad gave strict orders: "For tonight no farther than ankle deep, you hear? Stay together, and no going beyond sight of the house. New rules tomorrow—and church."

"My grandparents will be there," I added.

Dad headed for the steps to the deck. "I'm going to bed. Mess with my night's sleep, men, and pay the consequences. Get the groceries in." He sailed up the steps in three strides and disappeared into the house.

The beach house wasn't much to look at. As you come in, there's a round maple table with four chairs. The living room to the left is only big enough to hold two old stuffed chairs and a secondhand couch which backs up to the picture window overlooking the deck. A counter with bar stools opens into the galley kitchen. The bunkroom, bathroom, and Mom and Dad's room are down a short hall.

We unloaded the car and made our bunks. Beach gear we stored under the house on a dirt floor. We messed around in the dark surf awhile, then turned in. I opened the window in our room so we could sleep to the roar of the waves. As I dozed off, I heard Robbie sniffling.

# Chapter 8

IT was a gray morning; the ocean and sand were the same color. We threw on shorts and went wading in the foamy skim. The water was cold, but it didn't bother us. We made plans for the day and for sleeping on the beach. Robbie spotted the top of a lighthouse to the north. I said we could climb it later.

Dad was already up, jogging toward us from the direction of the lighthouse. "Rested up?" he asked.

We said we were.

"I'll be gone a few times this week—things to do, people to see. Here's the safety lecture." We gathered around. "The continental shelf is wide and shallow here, causing seven-foot tides. Riptides and undertows: don't mess with 'em, men. You'll think you have 'em, but they'll have you. Can you swim?"

"Yeah," Elijah said.

I said to him, "He means in the ocean. That's no camp swimming pool out there."

"I haven't swum in the ocean since I was little."

"Wingate?" Dad asked.

"Some," he said with no enthusiasm. I couldn't believe Dad was letting him get by with the stinking attitude.

"Buddy system, understand what I'm saying?"

We nodded.

"Let's get breakfast," he said.

We hauled driftwood out to the surf to watch it roll back in, picked up shells, and threw dead stuff at each other. Robbie found a sand dollar, but called it a sea biscuit.

"It's a sand dollar," I explained.

"It's a sea biscuit," he insisted.

"Settle it, Dad," I said.

He took the gray disc in his hand. "This is a sand dollar. *Sea biscuit*'s another word for 'hardtack': sea rations made of flour and water. Later on I'll tell you a legend about the sand dollar. You should leave that one alone, Wingate. See the fuzz on it? It's alive. Let it go or it'll die, and you'll be dealing with a handful of black slime."

Robbie flung it back into the sea, disgusted. The three of us took off running again.

"I can use this driftwood to make a huge fire tonight. I mean huge!" Elijah said.

"You a pyromaniac or something?" I asked.

"Not sure if a beach fire is legal," Dad told him. "I'll ask around. Get your duds on while I cook up breakfast. And brace yourself for some Pente*coastal* worship!"

We drove out of the jungle, off one island and onto another. Fifteen minutes later we pulled up to a little white building with a few cement steps, plain amber windows, and a steeple with a cross on it. A gigantic live oak tree shaded the whole gravel parking lot.

We were a little late. Inside, the swaying and lurching, the crying and praying were already going on. Grandma stood in the second row in a yellow suit. Grandpa was in a brown suit with a wide striped tie. They took time out from their swaying to turn and wave and blow kisses at us. We slipped in the back row. Dad leaned over and whispered to us, "Listen and learn."

People closed their eyes and murmured in languages that could have been English or Gullah, or something else. I couldn't tell. I hadn't been to church here for a while, but it felt homey. The minister stopped for an announcement: somebody had died and people were needed to come together to supply money for the funeral, food, and comfort for the bereaved.

A choir from another church took most of the time, singing songs about wheels of fire, the mighty kingdom, Ezekiel's dry bones, and power in the blood. During most of the singing, everyone stood. Elijah followed my lead and tried swaying and clapping. Robbie sneered and joined only after Dad gave him the evil eye. They were stiff as boards. Glancing down the pew at them, Dad shook his head and muttered something about zombies with arthritis. When everyone clapped and hollered at the end of the next song, Dad lifted his eyes to the ceiling and boomed, "Oh, Lord, forgive their whiteness!" I laughed out loud and he elbowed me. There was a sly twinkle in his eye, but he didn't crack a smile.

The church service was way cool. I was with my own kind for a change, while Robbie and Elijah were getting a taste of being odd men out, racially speaking.

The sermon was short because of the choir concert. The preacher punched the ends of his words with *uh!* "On the day we lost sister Esther-*uh,* she was tending the sick-*uh!* Ohhhh, who-*uh,* who will rise up to fill her shoes-*uh!?*"

Robbie bit his lip to keep from laughing, keeping a wary eye on Dad, afraid of getting pounded on the head.

After church Grandma and Grandpa loved on us and invited us for lunch. We followed Dad out to the car.

"How 'bout that?" he asked the guys. "What did you think?"

Robbie looked annoyed. "Okay, I guess."

"Elijah?"

"Why did that preacher keep saying *uh* at the end of every other word?" he asked.

Dad shrugged. "Finesse."

We didn't know what it meant, but we let it go.

There were lots of posh resort areas around the islands, but Grandma's house wasn't in one of them. My grandparents lived in a settlement of cottages and house trailers in a stand of tall scraggly pines. Their backyard dropped off into the backwater banks of the intercoastal waterway, which Elijah thought was a marsh.

Grandpa explained, "It's low tide, boys. Boats come in and out at high tide."

The settlement was junked up with lawn ornaments and boats and boat trailers, a cool kind of junky. Everyone was relaxing out in their yards in lawn chairs or working on their boats. The clay-colored sky had turned aqua during church. It was warm and breezy and sunny.

Grandpa invited the neighbors to come eat. People and dogs came to the backyard and hung around the grill until the fish and chicken were done. Everyone pitched in food, and Grandma spread it out on the picnic table: beans and rice, barbecue, greens, noodles, brownies, and peach cobbler. We ate like starving prisoners.

The little kids played with the dogs. The adults talked about azaleas, how to make the best bait balls, the lack of good work on the islands, and sister Esther's "liftoff."

Grandma made us sit and digest, and then we played catch until Dad was talked out and ready to leave.

On the way back, Robbie was in good enough spirits to mimic the preacher, using Dad's Gullah accent: "Sista Estah-*uh*, she had ha liftoff jes befo day clean-*uh!* She not yah! She ride Ezekiel's chariot wheels to da sky! Pu-raise de Lawd hyah! *Uh!*"

He had us in stitches. Even Dad guffawed—and he's a hard nut to crack.

When we got back to the beach house and changed

clothes, Dad said, "Another rule, men. See that tree?" He
pointed to a crusty pole sitting by itself in a foot of seawater.
"If you can see that tree, you're in my sights." He sat his
high-powered binoculars on the window sill. "I can count
your nose hairs from here if you stay in sight of the tree at
all times. The exception is the lighthouse. I can't see you
there, but when the staff's on duty, you're free to explore the
grounds. It's historical; learn something. The view from the
top is . . . well, you'll see." He nodded toward the sea. "Waist
deep today and buddy system, understand what I'm saying?"

We nodded.

By the time we'd covered the beach a mile in each
direction, the lighthouse had closed for the day. We decided
to go first thing tomorrow. Elijah got busy dragging up
enough driftwood and palm fronds and pine needles to roast
a herd of pigs.

"Hot dogs," I explained to him. "That's our dinner
and they're already cooked. We just blacken the outsides.
*Comprende?*"

"It's dry tinder; it'll go up quick," he defended, and
proceeded to make more piles. He found plastic trash bags
in the house, tore them into flat pieces, and covered the
piles. "In case it rains," he explained.

"Pyro," I muttered, and went combing the beach for
good shells to take back to Mom. The powerful tide had
crushed most of them to powder.

Robbie spotted sets of tracks and wondered what they were.

"Hey, Nature Boy," I called to Elijah. "Can you read tracks?"

"I'm pretty good." He dusted sand from his hands and came over.

I went to where Robbie was and pointed to sets of three slashes heading toward the water. "What are these?"

"Bird."

I huffed. "You're not looking at an idiot. What *kind* of bird?"

His hands made the shape of a big cheeseburger. "About this size. Probably a tern."

"That was too easy," I said. "You've seen them flying around."

"You asked, City Boy," he teased.

"I'm a country boy. Lots of *different* countries. What are these?" I nodded to more scratchings in the sand.

"Small dog, short stride. A dachshund or Chihuahua."

Robbie said glumly, "Easy again."

"Well, you're not going to find anything else. No mountain goats, no buffalo."

"Oh yeah? What kind are these?" I pointed to another set of strange tracks, half doglike, half chicken scratch.

He knelt down, studied them, and said to himself, "This one is deeper, and the others . . ." He shook his head, baffled. "Uneven. Doesn't make sense."

"Stumped?"

He wasn't giving up. "This one is swirled like the foot went down then twisted. See, it repeats that way over and over." He followed the tracks until they faded into the tide.

"Come on, Nature Boy," I teased.

After a minute, he stood up, confident. "It's a three-legged dog, big, probably a Lab or collie."

I snorted. "Right. What color?"

"Chocolate."

"Sure? Bet money on it?" I dared him.

"I'm sure about everything but the color. No way to prove it though. He may not come back."

I shrugged. "Whatever. Speaking of feet, yours are big, you know that?"

"I'm going to be tall," was all he said, as he turned and walked away.

You can hardly fluster that kid. He has a natural, lonely kind of cool.

# Chapter 9

**DRY** palm fronds rattled in the wind behind the beach house. Out on the darkening sea, shrimp trawlers were coming in for the night. To the side of the house, Elijah made a circle of driftwood logs for seats, and started a bonfire for charring our hot dogs.

Dad joined us and complimented Elijah's fire-making skills. "Good work, Creek. But keep it small. We're allowed a campfire, not a conflagration!"

We incinerated some hot dogs, and Elijah let the fire die down because the wind was blustery. When he had a nice bed of coals, we roasted marshmallows. We sat around listening to the crackling fire, the roaring surf, and the wind blowing through the palms.

Dad stood. "You men gonna sleep out here?"

"We were thinking about it," I said.

Robbie shot me a hateful look. "Since when?"

I'd had it with his attitude. "Hey, spoilsport, it's a free country. You can sleep with the fishes for all I care!"

"Watch your mouth, Marcus," Dad said. He took a couple of steps, stopped and turned. "You know to gauge your camp according to the tide, I guess."

Once again he headed for the house, but stopped a second time, as if he remembered something.

"Oh, by the way, don't let de hag ride ya."

Elijah looked at me for a translation. I shrugged. *"No entiendo."*

"The boo hag," Dad said in a sinister voice. "Haven't heard of her?" He grinned wickedly and took a seat. "You need to know, men, if you're going to be out here alone tonight . . . she's a legend born in the misty swamps from the days when the Gullah practiced voodoo, living in the terror of darkness, shunning the power of the light. Boo hags are worse than vampires," he said in a low voice. "They don't suck your blood. They steal your breath. Ohhhh . . . they are the most frightful of all creatures from the abyss. Worse than a goblin or banshee, far, far more terrible than any apparition ever seen . . . living or dead."

Dad leaned in, his dark skin reflecting the deep red of the coals, his eyes dancing with flickering flames. I glanced at Robbie and Elijah. I hadn't seen their attention so glued since we found Kate Dowland at the bottom of the well.

"Boo hags have no skin," Dad said. "They are raw and red, grotesque beyond belief. They borrow the skin of a victim and hide in it, looking for their next victim, and then the next, and the next. Wingate, you see anyone walking along the beach today? Coulda been a boo hag, checking you out to see if you're a good fit. If they choose you, it's good-bye. And a wretched way to go it is!"

He paused. Our breathing stopped.

"But maybe . . . maybe . . . the boo hag just wants

to ride you, to steal your breath." He rubbed his hands together eagerly. "Here's how she'll do it. She'll fly around in her borrowed skin until she finds you. Then she'll lie in wait until it's dark." He looked around at the sky, nodded approvingly. "Like now. Yeah, it's plenty dark now. Then while you're sleeping, she'll slip out of her stolen skin, sneak in through a keyhole or a crack in the window." He paused again, looking around as if he just then realized where he was. "Of course, if you're sleeping on the beach, she won't have to bother with keyholes. You'll be out in the wide open. Free and clear. Anyhow, then as she takes your breath, you'll sink into helpless nightmares." He raised his finger and pointed at us one by one. He moaned, "Ohhh, there's a chance you'll survive, but you've got to know the key."

He glanced to the left, then to the right. "Here's the key, men: sleep through the ridin' if you can. If you see her sweeping through the air or hear the clicking of her hungry teeth, just sleep through it. Oh sure, you might wake up later—weak and tired and terrified—but at least you're alive." He gave each of us a hungry stare.

He was my dad, Dom Skidmore, I knew that. But for a flickering moment, the way his teeth gleamed in the firelight, I found myself wondering if he . . .

"I know what you're thinking," he said. "You're asking yourself, *What if I don't sleep through it? What if I wake up while the boo hag's ridin' me, stealing my breath?* Here's the answer to that. Heads up, men, this could save your life:

don't struggle, whatever you do, oooohhh, *whatever you do,* don't give her any trouble and she might spare you . . . to use you again . . . another night."

Suddenly he ducked, as if something had swooped over him. The three of us jumped. He sighed in relief. "Whew. Just a bat . . . I guess. Though I don't usually see bats out here this time of night. It's a little late for bats. Well," he stirred the coals, "while you're here on the island—on this lonely island at the edge of civilization, at the brink of a continent with nothing behind you but the jungle, nothing before you but the vast, eternal sea—sleep soundly, men. Sleep to the roar of the waves, to the dry palm branches rattling like Ezekiel's bones comin' to life, rattling like the clicking teeth of the boo hag. And if you wake up and a bloodred boo hag is hovering over you, don't struggle! Nooo . . . don't . . . move . . . Don't scream!!" He leaned farther in over the coals like a demon feeding off the flames. "Just . . . go back . . . to sleep. . . ."

He got up in one silky motion and went into the house.

The three of us sat there for a good minute. I forced out a chuckle.

Robbie turned to me, pale as a ghost. "Your dad," he said in a low, quivering voice, "is a psycho maniac."

As we made our pallets with hardly a word between us, I got an inkling that maybe the Get Down was boot camp, and our training drills were going to be lessons in raw fear.

# Chapter 10

THE next morning we woke up on the beach, stiff and salty. The suspense had wound us tight as drums. Groggy and wrung out—the symptoms of boo hag visitations—we crept into the house. Dad was gone. He'd left instructions about breakfast and a phone number where he could be reached.

We took showers to get rid of the itch of salt and sand, put on clean clothes, and headed for the lighthouse.

The lighthouse was a big swirl of red and white, like a candy cane. Towering above the tallest palm tree, it stood stark against the blue sky. The guys were impressed.

Around the base, bolts the size of a man's fist lashed nine-inch thick, steel-plated brick walls to the concrete foundation. We were admiring the bolts when behind us a voice crackled, "This baby's not going anywhere."

She was in men's trousers and a plaid shirt. Her hair was gray and short, her eyes small and squinty, her smile like a grimace. And though she was friendly enough, I couldn't quite get the words *boo hag* out of my head.

The lady—obviously the caretaker—patted the tower. "Yep, she's lasted through thirteen big hurricanes and quite a few earthquakes; she's good for that many more."

She unlocked the door, and we climbed the steep circular steps to the top.

Gray sand beaches circled the lighthouse park. To the south was the jungle, the dunes, and cabin rooftops beyond. Masts of boats moved along the channels of the intercoastal in the distance.

Elijah and I wanted to live up there. We talked about how we could fish by day and cook over a driftwood fire. At night we'd sleep safe above boo hag radar. We'd be untouchable.

"That's a dumb idea!" Robbie said. He watched the gulls and sulked. I think his mind was on the raven's curse.

While Elijah was distracted by the view, I slipped in front of Robbie, looked down at him, and rumbled, "Quit messin' up my vacation, Wingate."

What he said back I can't repeat.

When we came down, the caretaker was waiting for us. She peered past the lighthouse out toward the sea, winked one squinty eye at the sky. "Eerie."

"What?" I asked.

"When it's quiet here, that usually means all heck is breaking loose out there." She tossed her head toward the sea. "Don't know what Evelyn is doing. She's building."

"Evelyn?"

"Tropical storm. Heading this way, a few days out. You may have to evacuate."

Elijah led us back to the beach. "The waves have picked up since yesterday."

Robbie ran out and dove into a wave. He came up sputtering but dove into the next one, and the next.

"What's he doing?" I asked.

Elijah shrugged. "Swimming, I guess." We watched him for a minute. He wasn't having fun; he was working at it.

Elijah's eyes never left his cousin.


Dad took us fishing off Beaufort dock that afternoon. But the waves were so rough, we had no luck. Because of the wind, we couldn't build a fire. So it was canned stuff over the stove for dinner. Robbie brooded the whole time.

After dark Elijah and Robbie played cards. Dad went out on the deck, sat on a lawn chair, and stared into the night. I followed him out there. I had shells for Mom lined up on the deck rail. I looked them over.

"Thanks for taking us fishing," I said.

"You did good."

"Robbie's being a pain," I said. "He's kind of ruining it for Elijah and me."

"I know," Dad said.

"This isn't turning out like I thought."

"Got it. Hey, let me see that shell."

I handed him the one I was looking at, the best one of the lot, and waited for him to tell me what he was going to do about Robbie. He crushed the shell with his bare hand.

"Hey, what'd did you do that for?! Those are for Mom!"

He handed it to me. It was shattered, the whole side cracked open showing the inside. "You know about the golden mean?"

"No," I said and I didn't care.

"See that chamber there, where the sea creature lives, see how it coils in a spiral?"

"Yeah," I said, still not caring. It was the best of my shells.

"It is constructed on a precise mathematical formula, based on the fraction 1.618. How do you explain that?"

Another of Dad's questions with no answers.

"I don't know."

He went on. "The same math that applies to this," he pointed to the shell, "applies to the shape of galaxies, and to the proportions of your face. And to the patterns in some plants. How do you explain that?"

"I said I don't know."

"Design," he answered.

"So what's your point—and are you going to get me another shell like this for Mom, since you busted mine?"

"A design means there is a designer, son." He looked out on the sea. "See those waves? The curl of those waves is the same as this shell." He put the broken shell in my palm and pointed to the coil inside. "Do you get my point?"

I raised my eyebrow at him. "I'm supposed to?"

He pointed to the stars. "It's all about architecture. Design. A plan. He has a plan."

"Does that plan include Robbie's ruining my vacation?"

Dad laughed. "Maybe."

"Great," I snorted. "Just great."

# Chapter 11

ELIJAH and Robbie were already gone when I woke, just after day clean. I jogged down to where the beach curved back toward the mainland. There stood Elijah thigh deep in the rolling waves, bracing against the roaring tide. He was looking out to sea. I followed his look. Far out and up to his chest was Robbie, facing the sunrise.

Elijah caught my movement out of the corner of his eye. "I'm keeping watch," he said.

"How long has he been out there?"

"I don't know. He was already gone when I got up." His eye didn't leave his cousin.

I snorted. "So much for the buddy system. Has he moved farther out?"

"No, but the waves are getting rougher. A couple of times he had to jump to keep on top of them."

Coming down the beach was a big man in shorts and a sweatshirt. He strolled along slowly. At the end of a leash limped a large, chocolate Labrador retriever hobbling on three legs. I couldn't believe my eyes.

I chuckled at Elijah. "The next time the Brills call you Nature Boy, you should thank them. You're seriously cool."

He clenched his jaw against a grin and tried to act like he wasn't impressed with himself. But he was.

We nodded hello to the man and his dog making strange tracks, and went back to lifeguarding Robbie.

Elijah asked, "Hey, um, what were you and your dad talking about out there last night?"

"Not much. Why?"

"Just that I got up to get a drink, and Robbie went over to the couch by the window. I think he was listening. He didn't finish our game. He just went to bed."

"Hmm," I said casually, as I watched Wingate facing the great unknown. *This could be bad.* "He's going to burn his retinas if he keeps staring at the sun." I wasn't saying what was really on my mind.

"He knows better. Robbie's smart."

I started worrying. "We should get him," I said finally. "Hey, Wingate!" He ignored us. "I bet he can't hear us."

"He'll turn around in a minute," Elijah said hopefully.

I spotted a thread on the horizon wider than the ones before. I watched the wave approach, darker, taller than the others. Elijah had his eye on it too.

"That one there. Does that look bigger to you?" I asked.

"Yeah . . . way bigger." He looked at me. "Let's go!"

We fought the incoming waves, feeling the undertow pushing at our legs. We yelled Robbie's name, but he couldn't hear us. The moment he realized that he was staring down the big kahuna, he went stiff with fright. Coming at forty miles an hour, the wall of blue-green grew until it blocked out the horizon. Robbie hunkered down to chin deep, ready to spring. There was no way we'd reach him, but we plowed our way through the waves anyway. He timed his jump as best he could to meet the crest of the wave, but it was already in an eight-foot curl.

Robbie disappeared under that hurricane wave and fell into the churning grip of the undertow.

"Robbie!!!" Elijah screamed. The panic on his face was on mine too. We grabbed mouthfuls of air and jumped as high as we could. Then it was over us, hard and overwhelming. I came out on the other side, tumbling and struggling to find sand under my feet again. Its force had carried us back several yards. I sputtered and stood, looking around. No Robbie.

"Robbie!!" Elijah howled. His eyes, bloodshot and streaming salt water, said everything. It was his cousin's last moment, and he'd stood there and watched it happen.

A look passed between us, honest and raw: blame and guilt. We'd known what Robbie was thinking the day before: he'd been testing the waters, seeing what it would feel like to take on water, to go under and not come up. He'd overheard me complaining to Dad about what a downer he was, how he was ruining my vacation. He was going through the horrible time. I should have lightened up on him. But I didn't.

Elijah scanned the ocean, his face more hopeless with every wave. Too much time had passed. The sea, that old boo hag, had stolen Robbie's last breath. He was gone.

# Chapter 12

I turned back to the beach, scattered with bleached driftwood, white and gray and . . . something else white and black: a body in dark trunks.

"There he is!" I yelled.

We wasted no time, flailing arms and legs, using the strong surf to push us ashore.

Elijah stumbled to shore, dragged Robbie farther up on the sand, and fell to his knees. Robbie was white as a sheet, but at least he was breathing. He took air in gasps, fast and shallow, his eyebrows pinched in strain.

Again Elijah went into camp counselor mode. "You're okay, bud, you're okay. It was a hurricane wave. Big one. Huge one. We saw it coming, but you couldn't hear us. We tried to get to you, but wow—it was so huge! Here, roll over. Come on, spit it out, cough it out. You're okay."

Robbie spit and coughed up water for another minute until his lungs were clear. He rolled himself up into a sitting position. When Elijah got it that his cousin was going to live, he fell back on his heels, gray as the sand, speechless with relief.

I slapped him on the back, and said in my best Gullah accent, "Oona ain't oughta look yah amongst de ded people fa a man wa da libe, ainty? E da libe gin!"

Robbie sputtered, "I da libe gin?"

We all cracked up. I said, "Yassuh, you ain't had no liftoff, boy! You libe."

Eventually Robbie got to his feet, staggering at first, then straightening up. We headed back to the house. Suddenly he shot me a terrified look. "Don't tell your dad, Skid! Please don't tell him. He'll kill me!"

"Sure. But don't ever pull that stunt again, know what I'm saying?"

"Got it," Robbie said, nodding eagerly.

"Buddy system, got it?"

"Got it."

"We need you, Wingate," I said. "You're part of the alliance. You're one of the five." I said it, and I meant it.

Elijah said, "You know what I think happened?"

"Wingate almost ended up in Davy Jones's locker," I said.

He ignored me, turned to Robbie. "When Skid and I leaped up into the wave as it rolled over us, you must have washed right under our feet. That wave was so powerful, it canceled out the force of the riptides and undertows."

"Makes sense," I said.

When we got back to the house, Dad was gazing out the window, drinking coffee. His eyes were on the sea. His voice rumbled with rage. "I see you boys found yourselves a beached sea urchin."

Robbie froze. Steam rose from Dad's cup; he squinted at the sea as he took another sip.

I stammered, "Dad, we—"

Through clenched teeth he said, "Looked like it from here."

Robbie withered. "I'm sorry, Mr. Skidmore!"

Dad's eyes slid to Robbie, boring a hole right through him. He held up the binoculars. "You were out there alone, Wingate, alone in stormy surf. A wave from tropical storm Evelyn took you out. It had you, boy."

Robbie didn't answer.

Dad put down his cup and binoculars. "Didn't it?"

Elijah jumped in, "Yeah, but he—"

"Don't defend stupidity, Creek!"

He got up from the couch. All three of us backed against the open door. He came over and peered down at Robbie. "What were you thinking?"

"I was—"

"No, you weren't."

I knew better than to try to step in. One of us could take the heat, or all of us could be fried to a crisp. One or three. Robbie was on his own.

"There's a tree out there that needs to come down, Wingate. Could fall on the house in a storm. You're going to take it down."

"Huh?" Robbie asked.

"Yes, sir," Dad instructed.

"Y-yes, sir," Robbie repeated.

Dad went back to the couch and stared out at the sea. We fixed breakfast like we were in high church, whispering, careful not to talk loud or clatter dishes, sure we'd be thunderstruck if we stepped out of line.

The phone rang. Dad answered it. It was Mom. Just like that he went to mush, gushing, "Miss you, baby," murmuring low with his hand over the mouthpiece. When Mom talked, he hung on every word.

My Dad is two men, and he can turn either one on or off like a faucet. When I was little I only saw the hot: the flares of temper, the fists through the wall, the slammed doors and rattling windows. But after the horrible time, there were big changes. Things cooled down, and we've been pretty cool ever since.

He hung up the phone, went out to the deck a minute, and watched the sea. He came back in and announced, "Change of plans; we're going shrimping today. If Evelyn bears down on us, we might have to leave. Time will tell. This morning I'll teach you how to make bait, throw a net, twist the heads off shrimp and de-vein them." He looked at Robbie. "Frogmore stew's for dinner, if we don't get rained out. We'll take down that tree later." He stretched and roared out a yawn. "Get ready to chew some shrimp net!"

If we'd hated the idea, we wouldn't have dared to say so.

Elijah and I got KP duty while Dad took Robbie for a long walk. Heading out the door, Robbie glanced at us, his face slack with despair, like he was walking his last mile.

They were gone almost half an hour. When they came back, Robbie's eyes were red, but he looked okay otherwise.

# Chapter 13

ON the way to the shrimp dock, Robbie sat up front—
Dad's orders.

A friend of Dad's had a dock off the intercoastal. He
showed us how to make bait balls from stuff that looked
like cornmeal and smelled worse than roadkill. He swore it
would work. "You'll have Frogmore stew for dinner, boys, or
I'll eat this bait ball!" He dropped it in at the water's edge.

Robbie said, "Does the stew have frogs in it? 'Cause if it
does, I may not eat it."

"Frogmore's the name of a town, Wingate. If you like
shrimp, you'll like the stew."

Dad taught us how to throw our nets to make a circle:
"Imagine throwing a big, limp pizza crust. Take one edge
in your teeth, the other in your hand, and just swing it out
there, letting go with hands and teeth at the same second.
It's an art, so don't get discouraged. It'll take quite a few
tries. You want the net to spread into a nice circle on the
water, like so." He put a section of the net in his teeth and
gripped another section with his hands. Then he flung the
net. It landed perfectly. "Nice oval," he said proudly, "pretty
good. The weights around the edge of your net will sink it;
you pull it in and with any luck you'll have a shrimp or two."

All morning at the dock, Elijah and I wanted to ask Robbie what happened on the walk, but Dad hardly left his side. I told Dad about Elijah and the three-legged dog. He was impressed. Nobody brought up Robbie's near-death experience.

When we had a full bucket of shrimp, Dad showed us how to de-head and de-vein them. We worked hard until past lunch. Dad drove us back to the beach house at midafternoon. Elijah made a fire, I peeled vegetables, and Robbie hauled water for the big kettle and got the spices. In another hour we had Frogmore stew.

It rained from late afternoon to evening. One by one we fell asleep all over the house. By dark, the roar of the ocean had quieted. Evelyn wasn't going to make landfall. She veered north toward Maryland and was losing power.

The evening sun came out low over the jungle. The sky was streaked with red; the ocean breeze turned cool. Dad said. "Okay, Wingate, let's take down that tree."

Hanging like a loose tooth, the dead palm wasn't really close enough to be a danger. But this wasn't about the tree. It was about Robbie.

"Wingate, you'll climb. We'll add our weight to the trunk as it leans. Heave-ho until it comes down."

Robbie's round eyes traced the tree to top point, almost to the roof of our house, two stories off the ground.

"Dad," I said, feeling sorry for him. "He'll have to get pretty far up there to bring it down."

"We'll take turns hacking at the roots while he does."

*Like walking the plank.* I backed off, wanting nothing to do with it.

Elijah stepped up. "Uh—"

"Creek!" Dad snapped at him. "You got something you want to say!?"

"You're scaring him," he said bravely.

Dad went nose to nose with him. "Not as much as he's scaring me."

Dad looked over at Robbie. "When it starts to go, Wingate, you ride it down. I'll catch you. Got that?"

Robbie hesitated.

"What do you say?"

Robbie gulped, "Yes, sir."

"Let's get busy."

Robbie had a hard time. He put tennis shoes on, and Elijah and I walked him up the tree until our hands wouldn't reach.

"Bounce her," said Dad. "Go on."

Robbie was afraid to bounce too hard; either he'd be thrown off balance, or the tree would come crashing down under him.

"Get up there and help him out," Dad said to me.

"Let Elijah. He has good balance. He's a tree climber."

"You're the skateboarder." He frowned at me. I wasn't about to tell him about my new phobia. I'd work it out on my own time.

Elijah said, "I got a better idea." He stood up a long stick of driftwood for Robbie to grab onto. "This will steady you."

Dad hacked at the exposed roots with an ax; I used my tomahawk. Robbie got at ease holding onto the stick, so Elijah found a rope, threw it over the top of the tree and started pulling.

When we'd cut most of the roots, I got on the low end of the trunk, adding my weight, bouncing in sync with Robbie, working my way up little by little. We put our full strength into it. Dad egged Robbie on, saying, "Hang ten, Surfer Dude. Ride 'er out!"

Robbie finally started to enjoy himself. When the cracking and splintering reached a peak, Dad yelled, "She's coming down, Wingate!" He rushed up under the high end, but Robbie said, "I can do it!"

The taproot snapped and the tree came crashing down, slow at first, then in a rush. Robbie rode it to the last few feet, timing his jump to the exact second before it hit the sand. He leaped off, did a drop roll, and was up on his feet again. When the tree hit the beach, he let out a whoop.

"We've killed our food and our fuel!" Robbie said proudly.

"You the man, Wingate!" I said.

"Bona fide man," Dad said with a nod.

We pounded on Robbie and knocked him down just for sport. Dad rolled Robbie over with his foot, grinning at him. "Good work on that tree, Wingate. Let's wet our whistles. Name your poison: root beer? orange pop?"

That night I followed Dad out to the porch again. He was standing at attention toward the ocean.

"Night, Dad. We're beat."

He draped an arm over my shoulder. "Night, son."

"It was good what you did for Robbie today," I said.

"If things go down bad, he'll need to be tough."

"Yeah."

We stood there listening to the sea. "Couple more days," he said sadly.

"It's going fast."

"Miss your mom?"

"Yeah."

"Me too."

I turned to go in, but he held me fast. "Marcus, . . . let me say this." He cleared his throat and looked sort of nervous. "Son, I've . . . I've never said I'm sorry."

"What for?"

"You know."

He was talking about the horrible time, about our past.

"It's okay," I said.

"No."

Waves crashed. The only thing you could see out there were white lines of sea foam coming in, dissolving in the dark. Dad's broken voice came under the deep, pulsing rhythm of the sea. "Son, I am . . . so sorry."

He was meaning how he'd done the same thing to me that Robbie's dad was doing—leaving him high and dry.

"We made it though," I said with a lump in my throat. "We made it. That's what counts."

"Your mother's an amazing woman," he said, breathing in salt air. "To think I might have lost you both." His arm got heavy on my shoulder, but I liked it there. He pulled me closer to him.

We said nothing, watching the waves roll in, each one with a crash and then a hiss as it swiped at the shore, eating it away inch by inch.

"That's eternity out there," he nodded toward the dark horizon. "You never want to march into eternity without love. Not by accident, not on purpose. No way, no how."

I looked up and he was blinking. If a man like my dad cries, then it must be cool. If anyone ever says otherwise, I may have to break his face.

# Chapter 14

DAY clean. The week was winding down fast. We did everything over again: the lighthouse, hauling wood, hunting shells. Elijah gave Robbie and me archery lessons. We practiced throwing the tomahawk. Dad drank lots of coffee and sat on the deck making notes, drawing with markers and watching us—he was up to something.

Besides Frogmore stew, we'd been dining mostly on hot dogs and junk food. Dad missed Mom's gourmet cooking, so he treated us to a big dinner on the bay that night. We drove into the classy little town of Beaufort and got a table with a view of the intercoastal. The smell of sea salt and grilling steaks drifted on the air.

While we waited for our food, Robbie said, "Hey, I found a dead sand dollar." Pulling it out of his pocket, he accidentally broke it into several pieces.

Before he could complain, Dad said, "Perfect. I wanted to show you something." With his big hands, Dad delicately put the pieces together on the red linen napkin. "It tells the story of Jesus. On this side do you see the outline of five petals? It's a poinsettia, the Christmas flower. That represents the birth of Jesus. These five holes represent Jesus' wounds on the cross: his hands, his feet, and the one in his side." He carefully turned the pieces over and put them together again: "Here's the Easter lily, the resurrection flower. And when you break it open . . . " With a table knife he dug out five tiny white bones shaped like birds. "You find doves, representing peace on earth. Fit them together like so, and you have the star of Bethlehem."

"Wow. I've heard of that," Elijah said quietly, "but I'd never seen it before." He took the doves in his hand and studied them awhile. "Can I have these?"

"Sure," said Robbie. "I want a whole one to take back."

Elijah washed the little doves in his water glass and laid them on his napkin to dry.

"A present?" I asked.

He just looked at me.

"She'll love 'em."

On the way home Dad stopped at the bridge to the island. He ran down to the shore with a jar, scooped up a handful of mud, and washed his hands in the channel.

"What's that for?" I asked.

"It's pluff mud. Those are oyster beds down there," he said, sliding in behind the wheel.

The car sat in the driveway most of the next day, but Dad was nowhere to be found. We spent hours building a sand castle, using driftwood as reinforcement. Elijah carved nicknames for us—Nature Boy, Sand Dollar, and Pluff Mud—into the center pole. The castle wasn't pretty, but it was big. We talked about sleeping on the beach again.

Elijah built one huge fire that night. A trawler miles out to sea could have spotted us. Dad made shrimp gravy and grits. We all brought out bowls and watched the fire while we ate. It was our last meal on the beach, and we were feeling it. I hadn't noticed until that moment how Robbie's mood had changed. He wasn't blubbering in his bunk at night, wishing to go home. He looked healthier, was working on a tan, and was standing taller.

Toward the end of dinner, Dad went into the beach house. He came back out in battle fatigues and a black T-shirt. His face was smeared with black mud.

My blood started pumping. "Uh-oh."

"What?" Elijah whispered.

"The Get Down," I said under my breath.

"Is that Gullah?" he asked.

"It's trouble, that's all I know."

Dad said, "Finish up, then get dressed in dark clothes."

We raced into the house, tossing our bowls in the sink.

"What's going on?" Elijah asked.

"Beats me," I said. I peeled off my shorts and threw on jeans. I had a dark T-shirt on already. Robbie borrowed my dad's black turtleneck, and Elijah had a navy T-shirt.

Dad had the jar of stinking marsh mud and made us smear it on our faces, arms, and the back of our hands. Around the fire we looked like dark savages, except for Robbie whose white-blond hair and blue eyes glowed. "You are seriously weird looking," I told him.

Dad had him go back in the beach house and get a sock cap to cover his head. He came back out, showing nothing but teeth and eyes.

"Oh, that's better," I said sarcastically.

"Quiet," Dad said. "Here's the drill. The one who wounds or captures the most enemies gets this." He showed us a wad of bills and then stuffed them into his pants pocket. He named us. "You're Vietcong," he said to me. He nodded at Elijah: "Navajo." He looked at Robbie. "You're Viking. You are each other's deadly foes, and mine." Elijah nudged me away and moved to the other side of the campfire.

"What's *your* code name?" I asked Dad.

"Metatron."

I laughed. "Oh, righteous! You're putting us through some kind of combat simulation."

"This is war," he said fiercely. He was getting into it big time. "You can still fight if you are wounded."

"What do you mean by wound or capture?" Elijah asked.

He pulled out a handful of peel-off badges and slapped them on our chests. "To wound your enemy, stick one of your badges on his back. A wounded soldier must then stay in his spot for exactly one minute before he can move against you. Best to stay still. You can be wounded by someone else while you're down. A smart soldier doesn't draw fire if he can help it." He handed us each a map and a penlight. "There's your battleground." He nodded toward the black jungle.

"You gotta be kidding," I said under my breath.

"After one minute has passed, you may move out again. If you wound the same enemy twice before he can wound you, he's captured, although you must let him get completely out of your sight before you pursue him again. You take one of his badges and wear it on your shoulder. A captured soldier must remain in his spot for five minutes. Once the five minutes is up, he may escape to hunt other enemies, but he can't pursue his captor. Be the first to capture all three enemies and win."

"It's impossible," Robbie said.

I was thinking the same thing. Elijah stared out to sea.

"If for some reason you lose any of the badges in your possession, it's a breach of security. You've lost, unless you can retrieve them."

"Double impossible," Robbie said looking bleak.

Dad wouldn't budge. "Not if you're a skilled combatant. Prepare."

We compared badges, each with our own logo: mine was a machete with the name Vietcong under it, Elijah's was an arrowhead labeled Navajo, and Robbie's was a Viking shield and battle-ax. "Metatron" was quite an artist. His badge had the silhouette of an angel with a sword.

"Anyone who gets captured twice—that is, by two separate enemies—must yell 'Navajo down' or 'Metatron down,' whatever name applies to you. You'll come back here and maintain the fire." He drilled each one of us with a look. "Only a stinking coward would intentionally get captured. Now, Viking, you start north at the fence near the lighthouse. But stay off lighthouse park property; it's off-limits after dark, and you'd get arrested. Navajo, start south at the dunes. Vietcong, go west to the stand of tall pines just this side of the swamp. I'll start at the beach side. You have a two-minute head start on me. Look at your maps. Don't get out of the marked area. Creatures of the night inhabit the swamp. Don't get eaten. Each of you gets a canteen. Okay, go."

Robbie said, "I don't know how—"

"Do your best," Dad snapped. In less than a minute, he'd disappeared in the trees.

"Wait! What about our head start?" I yelled.

We stuck on our badges and gathered our canteens. Robbie didn't want to go. I could see it in his black-rimmed, watery blue eyes. I felt sorry for him, wondering if Dad was pushing too hard. We Skidmores are pretty intense.

I ran to the beach house, filled my canteen full. I knew from Dad's military training that a half-filled canteen sloshes: a dead giveaway. On my way out, I noticed the phone flung on the couch, without its cord.

*Why would Dad disconnect the phone?*

# Chapter 15

I ran through the jungle to the western edge, near the swamp, which smelled of stagnant seawater and rotting plants. It made faint lapping sounds; swamp creatures splashed and gurgled. I fought off fear.

I'd played in the jungle before, but in daylight and never alone. The jungle floor was uneven, full of ruts and holes. I used the penlight for one last look at the map. I wouldn't be able to use it during combat. The others were a long way from my starting point, but I also knew how fast Elijah could run. I flicked off the light. Dots and patches of faint light flickered on waxy palmettos and scrub bushes. You couldn't tell what moved from what didn't. Everything *looked* like it moved, shiny and shifty as snakeskin.

I took a few steps, listened, took a few more. *No way to get into the thick of the jungle without making noise. Leaves crunch. Pinecones pop under my feet. The wind helps, rustling the palm fronds . . . like Ezekiel's dry bones.*

I moved toward the center, thinking I'd find a hiding place and wait for the others to pass. I wanted to win, but I was no idiot about my chances. Next to Dad, Nature Boy had the real advantage. Viking had zero. Nada. How was this supposed to help him? I hoped Dad knew what he was doing.

*Crack.* I whirled around, back toward the swamp. *Nothing there.* But someone *was* there, I knew it. I held my breath. A branch rattled in the wind and let go. I dodged it and ran from the noise, not wanting the others to discover me. I stopped often to get my bearings. *If Navajo has the same idea about getting to the center, we could crack skulls never having seen each other coming.*

I'd been in the heart of the jungle maybe a half hour—it felt like days—when I heard footsteps. I stopped, my heart pounding in my ears. *Slow down, heart. Slow down.*

It was Viking, moving south. He didn't know I was there. I circled around, taking steps with his so he wouldn't hear me. I was gaining ground. I reached for my badge to peel it off, so I'd be ready to slap it on him when . . . *whoosh!* Something sailed over my head! I ducked, curling myself under a scrub bush. *What was that!?* I looked up, but whatever it was had disappeared. Viking heard it and spun around.

Viking stared in my direction a long time. He whispered shakily, "Is that you?" I didn't answer. He backed up, turned, and ran. His footsteps faded.

*This is impossible! I'll never get close enough to anyone to stick on my badge without being detected. And what was that? A seagull? A tern? Do they even fly at night?*

I kept moving step-by-step, listening between each step. I was sweating in my jeans and T-shirt. There was a birdcall, a faint, high trill. Whether or not it was real, I didn't know. It sounded fake. It could have been Navajo trying to throw his voice. *What's he up to? Tying to lure me, or throw me off? Am I close?* I was dying to know, but I headed in Viking's direction instead, slow and steady, step-by-step. He'd be easier to wound.

*Thud!* I whirled around. Off to my right maybe thirty yards away, someone stood half hidden behind a tree. I melted behind a palmetto and watched him. He didn't move. *Is he watching me or facing the other direction?* Something skittered in the underbrush not far behind me, something small, like a squirrel. I ignored it, stayed focused on . . . who? It had to be Navajo. He was smaller than Dad. Robbie had gone in the other direction. Whoever it was wasn't moving a muscle. Only Navajo with his Indian skills could be that stone-still. Maybe he'd been wounded and was waiting out his minute. *I would have heard them talk, wouldn't I?* I moved toward the tree. *Quiet, quiet, closer, closer. He has no clue I'm here. Can't believe Nature Boy can't hear me. Maybe he sees something over there, toward the beach. Has he spotted Dad? Can't believe I'm actually wounding Nature Boy!* I peeled off a badge. *Quiet, quiet . . . almost there . . . easy, easy . . .* Heart racing, I reached out for his shoulder and slapped on my badge.

*Gross!* My hand landed on something wet and pasty. It wasn't sweat. Navajo didn't move . . . it wasn't him! It wasn't even human! I jerked my hand back.

*My mind raged, then suddenly cleared. Dummy. It's a dummy!*

My trembling fingers scrambled for the penlight. I found

the light in my pocket and flashed it on the face. I jumped back in horror. A hideous bloodred face! *A boo hag!*

Feelings shot through me like lightning: terror, disgust . . . then relief. And excitement! *A boo hag dummy! Oh, this is good, Dad! This is seriously cool!* I flicked off my light and laughed to myself. *Ketchup and pluff mud. Big sparkly doll eyes, no nose, plastic vampire teeth. Disgusting! Cool!*

The trees rattled in the wind. I heard a clicking sound. *I have cover of darkness and noise. I can move fast.*

Moving to a new position farther south toward the dunes, I was seriously determined to get Navajo.

I hid under a heavy shrub and waited, sure one of the others would come my way. Doubts and strange thoughts ran through my mind. Maybe this was all a big joke on me. The others were back at the house. They'd ordered pizza while I was out here by myself, sweating, rotting. *What's Dad trying to teach Robbie? Not to fear being alone? Not to give up? What else?* I sensed there was more. I kept hearing noises all around me: skittering and rattling, whirring and clicking too—unnatural sounds, and strange, birdlike calls.

The waiting unnerved me. The others might be doing the same, just sitting and waiting, perched in our spots all night; we'd never capture or wound anyone. No fun. I changed my strategy. I'd start a systematic sweep from one end of the combat area to the other. I drank my fill of the canteen, poured out the rest, and left the canteen there.

# Chapter 16

I headed toward the lighthouse, cutting straight through the center of the jungle. My eye caught something in the bushes. I had just passed someone . . . not moving— perfectly still. Who? I watched him, heart pounding. When he didn't move, I took a step toward him. No movement, another step. I aimed my penlight across the gully and clicked it on. I gasped in spite of myself. *Another boo hag! My heart thudded, but I had to chuckle. Oh, this is too sweet! I can't wait to hear Elijah or Robbie scream out in fright!* I kept my cool this time.

Every cell in my body was on high alert, buzzing and tingling. I was exhausted and fired up at the same time. Terrified and excited.

More time passed. An hour? I didn't know. A scream pierced the night.

*Sounds like Viking,* I chuckled to myself. *He's found himself a boo hag.* I headed toward the scream, hoping to capture Robbie while he was scared and distracted.

I was almost to the place where I'd heard the scream when I spotted a human shape, half hidden behind a palm tree, across a deep crack in the jungle floor. I ducked down.

*Good strategy, Viking!* I thought. *Scream, bring us running, hide and slap a badge on the first sucker that passes too close. Too bad it didn't work. I see you!*

He didn't look like Viking. He seemed bigger, more square-shouldered.

*Aha! Another boo hag, bigger and badder. Cool. What strategy now?*

I could make a noise and draw the other guys' attention. They would come, spot the decoy, sneak up to it, and then I'd move in for the kill.

I took a few steps toward the big boo hag. It moved. I stopped. *What?* Had my eyes fooled me, or was it the shifting light? *Okay. It's strung up on a string, swaying in the breeze. There is a breeze. Palms have been rattling all night, the clicking and—*

Its face moved into a patch of light, a dark face, its white eyes looking right at me. *Dad?* My heart jumped to my throat. My mind kept trying to make the creature into my dad, the shape of his head, the width of his neck.

"Dad?" I called out weakly.

This thing was much bigger than Dad. It was coming toward me, floating between the palmettos.

*Okay,* I told myself desperately, *he's rigged up a line or something. A big boo hag blowing along a fishing line.*

Its thick arms moved. It had hands, with moving fingers. It took a step, a heavy, crushing step. It wasn't a thing. It was human, alive . . . it wasn't floating, and it wasn't Dad! It leaped across a crack in the ground. *Crunch!*

*It's coming!*

I turned and ran for my life, my heart racing. *Is it following? What is it?! Do I turn on the light to see my way? No! Dead giveaway! If I yell to warn the others, it'll hear me! Run!! Where am I headed? Toward the lighthouse? Wrong direction! Get back to the house and lock the door, call the police—no, can't, the phone's disconnected. Dad unhooked . . . the phone. . . .*

I stopped, shot a look behind me. *No one there.* I listened. Nothing. *Dead calm.*

*Dad had disconnected the phone. But why?*

*Okay,* I said to myself, trying to keep my thoughts in a row, *what if the big guy's a plant, part of the game? And Dad knew we'd run home and call the police if we saw him. He wouldn't want cops out here messing with his game. Okay. So we're still in the game. It's just part of the simulation . . . isn't it?*

But what if it wasn't? Dad warned us not to wander into the lighthouse park, that we'd be arrested. *Was that guy a security guard? Wouldn't he have said "Stop!" or "Who goes there?"*

Something slapped my shoulder. I yelled out and spun around.

"Gotcha, Cong!"

*Navajo!*

"Game over!" he gloated.

I blurted out, "There's somebody out there! A huge guy."

"Good one," he said calmly. "Nice strategy. You're wounded. I get one minute."

"I'm not kidding!" I said.

"It's your Dad, Skid. I've been tracking him."

"It wasn't him!"

"He was rigging something up in the tree. It looked like a snake hanging down. Did you hear that yell before? I think Robbie ran right into it."

"This was a big, huge guy. Bigger than Dad. I'm telling you!"

Navajo wasn't convinced. "It won't work. You're stuck here for one minute. See ya."

My whisper became a cry. "Wait! I'm not lying, Creek! Don't leave!"

He heard the fear in my voice and turned back. "Shhh. Okay, where'd you see him?"

"Back that way, straight through toward the dunes. You've been tracking my dad? Where is he?"

I couldn't see Elijah's face, but his voice sounded unsettled. "For a while I did. But I lost him."

"How could you lose him? You're a good tracker."

"I don't know. He was there, then he wasn't."

Worry flooded my mind. *What if that creature got my dad?* "It's all part of the game, isn't it?" I said weakly, sweat dripping down my forehead.

We'd heard the whoosh of wings, heard twigs snapping and a *click, click, click*ing. But nothing was there! Elijah had tracked my dad and lost him. And Robbie, we figured, was heading toward the swamp. We made our way in that direction.

*Thud.* Something heavy fell nearby. Elijah and I dropped behind a bush. No other sound followed, nothing moved through the dim, moon-spattered jungle. He slipped from beside me. Like an animal he stalked the source of the thud. I stayed put. Twenty yards away, he stopped and bent to the ground. His penlight flickered on, then off. He motioned me over. "It's a big rock." His head shot straight up. "He's above us."

"Who?" I asked.

*Click, click. Clickety, click.*

"What *is* that!?" I hissed.

"Shh," he said.

A scream echoed through the trees and died quickly to a muffled moan, then faded to silence.

"That was Robbie!" I said.

Elijah took off. I followed, running when he ran, stopping on his cue to listen and to get our bearings.

"It was from there," I said, pointing toward the ocean.

"No, there," he said, pointing south.

Who was I to argue with Nature Boy? We went south. We paused to catch our breaths. *Click, click.*

I didn't know much about weapons, but it sounded like the click of a gun from up in the trees. Or the click of a boo hag's teeth. "Was that a gun?" I said.

"You're panicking," he said.

He took off again toward Robbie's last scream, leaping over the rough terrain, nimble as a deer. I stood there, unable to decide. *Should I go back to the beach house? Was the game over? Should I call out for Dad?*

Elijah was maybe fifty yards ahead, almost gone from sight when he stopped suddenly, bent down, picked something up.

"What is it?" I called in a loud whisper.

"Robbie's stuff. His canteen and light." His voice sounded small and far away and scared.

"Where'd he go?" I asked.

"He wouldn't drop his light," Elijah said. "He wouldn't . . ."

*Click, click, click.*

"What is that?" I asked. "I keep hearing that!"

From deep in the jungle came a wispy thing, sudden and huge and horrible, swooping through the trees. *Whoosh!* Elijah tried to run, but it descended over him, swallowing him whole. He and the thing disappeared into what looked like a deep trench, as if the thing had pulled him down into the earth, right down into Hades.

I stood there stunned. *It's part of the game, part of the game.* Not a sound from Elijah. *Why didn't he scream?* If anyone could get away, Elijah could.

*Where should I go? It's just a game! What should I do? It's just a game . . .*

*Click, click, click.*

Panic washed over me. I looked landward toward the swamp, toward the clicking. From the darkest part of the jungle, flying down at me from high in the trees, it came, swift as a bat, big and horrible, black as midnight. . . .

# Chapter 17

WE'D been bagged by boo hags and dumped on the beach by the fire.

By the time we could untangle ourselves, they were gone and Dad was beside us, roasting marshmallows.

The final score was sketchy: Elijah had wounded Robbie and me, and lost two of his badges. I'd lost one of my badges without being captured and had wounded no one. Robbie came out with one wound, and with one of each of our badges stuck on his cap, though he didn't seem to be aware of them.

"How'd *you* win?" I asked Robbie. I couldn't believe it.

He looked confused. "I kept hearing noises, but I couldn't see anything. I didn't get any badges."

"What do you mean?" I said. "They're on your head!"

When he got over the shock of seeing our badges stuck on his cap, he went into fits and threw the cap at Elijah. "Not funny! Just because I'm not Nature Boy—" He was so furious and humiliated, he gave Elijah a shove that rocked him back.

"It wasn't me!" Elijah yelled.

Dad smiled and nudged me. "That friend of yours—he knows his stuff . . ."

"It wasn't me!!" Elijah insisted.

"But he's not that good," Dad smiled slyly.

I couldn't believe it. "You did it, Dad? You helped Robbie win?"

Dad ignored us and got busy with the fire.

"Who were those other guys," I asked, "the boo hags?"

"You almost caught me, Navajo," Dad said. "Remember that gully where you tripped, where you laid low awhile and drank your water?"

"You saw me? Where were you?" Elijah asked in amazement.

"Why don't you tell them your tricks of the trade, Navajo? Indians are masters of stealth, aren't they?"

"Where *were* you?" Elijah persisted.

"You tell me."

"Above our heads?"

"Not fair!" I said. "There's no way we could have caught you. "Not fair," I mumbled.

"Did I *ever* say it was going to be fair?" Dad asked innocently. "Lesson One: Sometimes you get stuck in a game where others don't play fair. Life's not fair."

"So," I started. "Robbie really lost. . . ."

"His name is now Rob," Dad announced. "Lesson Two: If you acquire some intelligence that will help you live a better life, then you win. So you're all winners."

"*If* you survive it!" said the newly named Rob.

Dad tapped Rob's chest hard with his fist. "That— what's inside you there, your spirit—that will survive,

Wingate. It's eternal. Don't screw it up. Now, Navajo, tell us what you know. Tell us of the Indian ways."

Elijah sat down. "Well, I went barefoot." He stuck out his big ugly dogs, their soles black. "It's a lot quieter without shoes and you can feel twigs that may snap."

"Doesn't that hurt?" Dad questioned.

"A little. But I've been working on it. I've been through Telanoo barefoot a few times."

"Telanoo?"

"Code for The Land No One Owns," I answered. "It's Elijah's secret wilderness."

Dad grunted. "That so? I see. So if it hurts a little, that's okay, if you accomplish your goal. That's Lesson Three, and a good one. What else, Navajo?"

"If you can't see, then don't," Elijah said. "What I mean is close your eyes and let your other senses help you out."

"Good. Excellent. Use all your gifts and resources. That's Lesson Four. Keep going."

"I stayed downwind. Sound and smell travel on the wind."

"Hey, I don't smell!" I lobbed a stick at him.

"Yeah, you do. Wood smoke. When I knew we were doing combat, I eased you into the path of the campfire smoke."

Dad laughed now, shaking his head. "You are good."

"Also," Nature Boy was on a roll, "staring into the fire will blow your night vision, at least for a while. When you said we'd be doing night maneuvers, I quit looking at the fire. I looked out at the sea."

"So how did you get the badges, Dad?" I wanted to know. "You had hideouts set up beforehand, didn't you?"

He grinned. "I fess up. I scoped it out yesterday. Made a few perches along the perimeter of the open areas. Rigged some wires. I knew you'd want to stay under cover of darkness, but you'd want to be near the light to watch the others. You each thought the others would wander into the open, but of course, you all knew better. So you stayed to the perimeters of the bright areas. At one point, Marcus, you and Rob were no more than thirty feet apart and didn't know it." He dropped his head and chuckled. "I had night goggles too."

Elijah asked, "Who were the boo hags, the live ones?"

"You'll meet them tomorrow. Did they scare you?"

"Ridiculous question," Viking said, but he was starting to smile and admire the badges on his cap.

Dad said, "There was nothing to really be afraid of out there. Boo hags aren't real. And you had to know I unplugged the phone for a reason: I was up to something. So, Lesson Five: Some fears are real, but most are created in your own mind. Know the difference. And Lesson Six: War has rules. But in the end war is not about rules or badges. Winning a just war is about love; good men fight only when they have to, to defend those they love. Navajo, Vietcong, when you thought there might be real danger, you forgot about winning over each other and went into rescue mode. See, a man might know warfare by the book.

But without courage and integrity, he's lost the battle."

It was past 3:00 in the morning when we finished marshmallows and went back into the jungle to take down Dad's game setup. Elijah was in awe at the gear strung up in the jungle. "You went to a lot of trouble!"

"Oh, I needed a refresher course," Dad said. "Always good to keep the reflexes on alert."

Even together and with flashlights, we thought the wind-dried boo hags were seriously freaky. We retraced our paths and hunted down canteens, each telling his side of the story.

"I knew you were tracking me, Elijah," Dad said. "I was leading you away from Marcus's encounter with the bigger boo hag. I knew where each one of you was every minute."

"How?" Elijah asked.

"I had my angels posted. We communicated with walkie-talkies using clicks and birdcalls, a code we worked out."

He asked Dad, "So when I was on your trail, you'd throw the rocks to distract me?"

Dad nodded. "Or I'd yank off a branch and drop it, anything to divert your attention. And there's another lesson for you. Lesson Seven: When the enemy's on your heels, learn how to throw him." He nudged Elijah's skinny arm. "A couple of times you almost had me, Navajo. I have to tell you, you have a gift. A real gift."

When we reached the beach again, Dad turned to Rob. "Final lesson, troops, but especially for Viking here." He nodded at Rob, as we were ordered to call him now.

"Rob," Dad said solemnly, "that jungle out there, it can be terrifying. But here's Lesson Eight and don't forget it: Someone you can't see is helping you."

Rob said, "Yes, sir."

Dad clamped a hand on his shoulder and said, "You on de auction block, boy. Devil's biddin on you. He's callin' out a price. But you tell 'im you ain't fo sale! You a free man!" Then he reared back and roared, "God's chillun, dey like de angels! An dem angels outta heaben gwine to hep de boy!" He laughed so big and hard, we laughed too.

My dad's wired differently. Nothing I can do about that. Back at the beach house, Rob said cautiously, "So I won?"

"Looks like it," Dad said.

"What about the money?"

"No money," Dad said.

"Then . . . you cheated me," Rob said, backing up.

"War's not fair," Dad said. "Lesson One."

Robbie looked at me. I shrugged. Nothing I could do.

Dad tossed us mugs from the kitchen cabinet. We made hot chocolate, and it was the best we'd ever had. We ate up the rest of the Frogmore stew for early breakfast. We showered off the mud and sand.

"Get some shut-eye, men," Dad said. "We're moving out at nine hundred hours."

# PART 3: THE STORM

*His way is in the whirlwind and the storm,
and clouds are the dust of his feet.*

—Nahum 1:3

# Chapter 18

EIGHT hundred hours. The phone rang.

"Get that!" Dad barked over a skillet of bacon: second breakfast. I staggered out of bed and into the living room. "Probably your mom, calling to see if we've left yet."

I grabbed up the phone. A girl's voice said, "You'll never guess in a million years." It was Reece.

"Does that mean you want me to guess?" I asked.

"I don't know. Do you want to guess?" she asked excitedly.

"No."

She huffed into the phone. "Is Elijah there?"

I held up the phone. "It's for you, Nature Boy!"

Elijah got up from the couch, scratching his head and trying to wake up. He'd slept all night under the open window. He reached for the phone, eyes still closed.

"H'lo." His eyes popped. "Hi . . . yeah, oh yeah, the greatest time! What? I don't know, what? . . . Just tell me." He perked up. "No kidding!" He turned to me. "She has Dowland's journals. There're a lot of them!" He sat down on the couch, intent on what Reece was telling him. "Yeah? What do they say?" He was shocked. "Really? Like what?"

Rob appeared in the hallway. "What's going on?"

"She says his journals talk about me." Into the phone Elijah asked, "What does it say? What about the armor? . . . Well, flip through some pages. See if you see anything." He turned to us. "She just got them a few minutes ago. There's a whole stack. She's going to read a page."

Rob and I leaned our ears to the phone.

Elijah said, "Talk loud, Reece. We're all listening."

"Hold on," she said. "There was this one page . . . one of the few things I could understand, sort of. Let's see if I can find it again . . . okay, okay!" she cried. "In one of the books, he has a list of stuff and then your name written and crossed out a couple of times."

"What's that mean?"

"I just got them, for crying out loud."

In a take-charge way Elijah said, "Okay, keep going through them. Write down stuff that makes sense. We'll get in late tonight—"

"Tomorrow," Dad interrupted.

"Tomorrow," Elijah repeated, but I'll see you Monday. Are the journals ours?"

Reece answered. "We can't keep them, but we're free to look. I'm at the police station." Then her voice went to whispers, but we caught the gist of it: the police department had hit a snag. They wanted our help.

"Cool," Elijah said.

She mumbled something that made his face red.

"I will," he said in a hush, then cleared his throat and said in his regular voice, "I mean, we will."

"What'd she say, Creek?" I asked.

"Nothing." His eyes shifted to the floor.

"She misses you, darlin', and hurry back?"

Elijah covered the mouthpiece with his hand and scowled at me semi-fiercely. "Dry up . . . Pluff Mud."

"Name-caller." I had to stop the mush before it got out of hand. I grabbed the phone. "Hey, Reece. It's me again, so don't say anything you'll regret. About those journals— good going, girl!"

Mei's voice spilled in. "Hi, Skid!"

Elijah yelled into the phone, "Bring your notes to school on Monday!"

"Hey! Don't hang up," she said. "That's not all!" She said something, but I couldn't understand it. Elijah jolted again. He shot a look at me. "The police are going to dig up the body in the reject grave!"

It was hard to leave the beach and the ocean—the fun of killing our own food and fuel, running the beach, leaping waves, the jungle war games. I could have stayed forever, living the beach bum life. As we pulled out and the beach house disappeared behind the trees, Elijah kept looking back. So did Rob.

But life called. We had new info. This mystery of the armor was peeling like an onion, layer by layer.

"Thanks for the vacation, Dad," I said.

Elijah said, "Oh yeah, thanks, Mr. Skidmore. This was the greatest week ever."

Dad nodded and glanced over at Rob, whom he'd ordered into the front seat one last time. "How 'bout you, Rob Wingate?"

Rob's voice was deep with feeling. "I had a really, really good time."

Dad pressed a fist into his shoulder. "You go back and make your mom some Frogmore stew. How 'bout it, sir?"

"Okay, sir," he grinned.

Dad glanced back at me in the rearview mirror. A deep look passed between us. A feeling welled up in my chest, a feeling tough to explain. It was about Dad and me being who we were—military men, men of the sea and the Low Country, and of the wide world. All-American men, ex-slaves but free. Together no matter what.

A few miles inland, he pulled into a military base. "I said you'd meet your haunts."

They met us at the gatehouse. Peck had red hair, green eyes and a thin, freckled face. He was a little bigger than us guys. Dad was the in-between size; then came Yancy, six and a half feet plus, a mountain of black muscle, no neck, bulgy eyes, a big toothy smile—the kind of guy who could carry his whole family on his shoulders. We all shook hands.

Dad said, "Here you have us, men, your combat simulation boo hags."

Rob stared up at Yancy. "Thank goodness I never saw you! I would've died on the spot."

They roared. Dad slapped me proudly on the back. "I reserved that encounter for my boy."

"Thanks, Dad," I said. "You're a jewel."

Rob smiled. "Thanks for scaring us half to death. We really liked it." I couldn't believe my ears.

They said our first try at guerilla warfare was pretty good, and admitted to the challenge of staying one step ahead of Navajo. I told them how he decoded the three-legged dog tracks and how he hunts barefoot in the woods in the dead of winter.

We wanted to hang out around the base, but they had things to do. "Gotta get back to saving the world," said Peck.

"We're with you on that," I said.

The car windows were rolled down, the radio blaring sweet jazz. We replayed every day; Dad wanted to hear our war stories again from each viewpoint. He grilled us on the Eight Lessons again, saying they were good for life. I poked fun at his war game name. "What was up with Metatron?"

"It's just a made-up name, men. A mythic name I picked up in a discussion with the Stallards about their way-out research. Legend springs from fact, and this fact is stranger than fiction—it's about a man who never died."

"Nuh-uh," Elijah said.

"Fact!" Dad barked. "The seventh son from Adam was so righteous that he walked with God on the earth, and God took him straight to Heaven. He never died."

Elijah and Rob sat there doubting.

"In the distant past, men, mysterious things happened all the time; but the story of Enoch was so special, it was set down for all time. Why did such a man never taste death, ancient folk wondered? Enoch lived a righteous life—that was the simple truth of it. But wild truth breeds wild tales, you see. One myth had it that Enoch became God's record keeper, writing down all the deeds of men. Mystics named him Metatron. That's all I know." He chuckled. "You get on some pretty weird subjects with the Stallards. I just liked the name."

We zipped along above the clouds of the Blue Ridge, the wind crisp and clean. The smells of sea life were gone except for the bait ball stink that wouldn't wash off our hands. Feeling sad about losing the seaside life, we stuck our heads out the windows and howled like wolves. Even Dad did. Then he broke into a verse of "Oh, Shenandoah."

We drove into a little city, got drive-through lunches, and went to a park. We spread sleeping bags on the lawn and had a picnic. Dad finished his burger and fries and stretched out. "I'm going to need some sleep, men."

I teased, "What's the matter, Dad? Can't handle a little deadly combat and one measly sleepless night—"

"—and a twelve-hour deployment to the home front?

Yeah, I can handle it, if I have to." He tucked his hands behind his head, closed his eyes, and smiled. "But I don't have to. Not today. Mission accomplished." He winked at me. "I don't want to be a zombie when I get home to your momma. Bother my sleep, men, and pay the consequences."

We skipped rocks in the lake and walked a trail. The rest of the time we hung out flat on our backs watching clouds float by. Keeping his voice low so Dad wouldn't hear, Elijah tried to reel me in about my thing with Miranda Varner, but I didn't take the bait. "I can only tell you what Dad told me once," I said: "'Women, son—women are these china dolls packed with dynamite. Treat 'em careless and you could lose a hand.'" I added, "He's given me my specific orders about women, but that's between him and me."

Elijah and Rob half smiled.

Late that afternoon, Dad roused and we took off. The next thing I knew, it was the wee hours and we were pulling into Camp Mudj. Dad tossed some bills to each of us. "You earned it." I couldn't exactly tell in the dark, but there were lots of bills and they weren't just ones. He more than kept his word; he made us all winners.

# Chapter 19

MAGDELINE Independent felt ordinary on Monday morning. What a downer. We met at Elijah's locker in the middle hall. Mei ran up to us. One glance at Rob and her mouth dropped open. *"Sugoi! Genki desu ka?* You look very healthy!"

When Reece showed up, Elijah practically ran her over, grabbing her book bag so she wouldn't have to carry it the last twelve inches. Mr. Obvious beamed at her and acted like he didn't notice the crutch.

"There's a lot of stuff to tell you," she said. "The first few notebooks were full of notes for sermons, and things about his family tree, and some other stuff I couldn't decipher. There are lots of history notes, not to mention sections on geology and metallurgy. Skid, we're going to need the Quella too. There're a ton of Scriptures. And we need the Stallards."

"Metallurgy? Sounds like homework," I said darkly. "By the way, this guy's name is now Rob."

Reece and Mei shot him questioning looks.

His chin went up. "Yeah. I want to be called Rob now."

Reece said, "Sure, okay," then got back to business. "We didn't find any clues about the breastplate yet."

"We need a powwow," Elijah said.

Chapter 19

"How about at the police station?" I suggested. "Or, hey, would the cops let us borrow the journals, if a parent signed?"

"My dad would sign," Elijah said.

"So would mine," I said.

It got quiet. Here's where Rob would have said, "Mine too," but where his dad was, he wasn't saying.

Reece jumped in. "My mom's on an assignment in Pittsburgh, so she can't. I'm at Mei's for a few days."

I put up a hand. "Right, so okay, Elijah, ask your dad first. He and Officer Taylor are buds."

By the end of the day, Rob had begun to lose the healthy look he'd gained at the beach. I caught up with him in the hall and swung an arm around his neck. "Hey, Wingate, if we get the notebooks, how 'bout the powwow at your house?"

"Thunderstorms are coming today or tomorrow," he answered, being evasive.

"Exactly. We can't have it outside around one of Elijah's infernos. I say we get the notebooks, go to your attic, spread out, and not be bothered."

"The roof leaks."

"Who cares?"

He shrugged. "Okay with me."

"Done deal," I said, keeping the mood on the upswing. "The Castle it is. Being in a tower during a storm, that'd be awesome. We should have popcorn."

He got honest with me. "My dad won't be home. He moved out for good."

Whatever my parents had tried to do for Rob's parents over the week obviously hadn't worked. I braced myself to hear him singing the Wingate blues and said a prayer that his training in death waves, falling trees, and jungle boo hags would kick in. We headed toward the front door.

I gave him a couple of easy punches between the shoulder blades. "That stinks. Keep in mind, Viking, it ain't over 'til the fat lady sings."

He forced a laugh.

"Catch you later," I said.

# Chapter 20

THE attic was stifling that next evening when we gathered to get a look at the journals. Rob threw open the window to a quiet, eerie-looking sky. Reece pulled herself up the stairs wearing her souvenir: five white bone doves stuck on a navy ribbon around her neck.

I leaned over to Reece. "Nice necklace."

She grinned.

Elijah went to the window. "Have you seen the raven since you've been back, Rob?"

"No," he said.

"I'd forgotten about him," I said, clearing a place in front of the old couch to spread out the notebooks. "What's your fixation with that bird, man?"

"It could be a sign," Elijah said as he came back and joined us. "And I think I'm supposed to be watching for signs."

Rob said darkly, "The bird's done his damage."

We took a minute to admire the belt of truth, still mounted above the door. Reece spread out Dowland's journals, a short stack of old spiral-bound notebooks. "We can have only a few at a time," she said, "but there's a lot of gibberish to wade through. This one had the Elijah message. See, there's a list here. The lines are in different ink, as if he wrote them at different times." She read the list scrawled down the page:

*Three coverings of righteousness*
*Three witnesses and judgment by fire*
*A threefold cord*
*Three days swallowed,*
*three days dead . . .*

"Here at the bottom of the page Elijah's name is crossed out, written again, crossed out once more, and written a third time." She held it out for us to see the page:

~~Elijah~~
~~Elijah~~
Elijah

Elijah's face washed out to gray. "What's that mean?"

A chill went up my spine. "Looks like he was after you, man," I said.

"Why's my name there three times?"

I looked to Rob for an answer, "Your turn, Viking."

He studied the page. "A bunch of threes. That's all I see. Maybe he tried to cross *you* out twice, and was aiming for a third try." He looked at Elijah. "Like a hit list, except you're the only guy on it."

Elijah argued, "He tried only once . . . with Salem."

"Wait!" said Reece. "Remember the night we were all asleep in the lodge and you heard someone creep in?"

Elijah drifted back in time. "Yeah . . . cold air swept across the floor, like someone coming in and out the door. . . ."

Mei said, "Maybe he was going to kill you, and he chicken out."

I gave Mei a friendly punch. "Chicken out? Mei, you learned a cliché! Congratulations!"

She rolled her eyes. "I have to. American English!"

Elijah frowned at us. "Guys, this is serious!"

Reece got a far-off look. "I prayed the armor over us that night in the lodge."

"*Prayed* the armor?" Rob asked.

"Yeah. I prayed that we would be protected by each of the pieces."

Elijah asked, "You can do that?" and before she could answer, he asked, "Does it work?"

"It's spiritual protection, not physical," she said bluntly. "Dowland still could have killed you. For it to work you have to believe, not in the armor—in God."

The light in the attic changed to a gray-green.

"It's getting dark already?" I asked. "It's not even 7:00."

"So what good is the prayer?" Elijah asked. "What good is armor if it can't protect you?"

Reece huffed. "If you want to be safe from sinning, and if you to want be ready when bad things happen to you, it can protect you in that way."

Rob had been listening with his arms crossed. "Your prayers didn't save me," he said gloomily. "I wasn't ready for the bad things to happen."

"Getting there, Wingate," I said. "Stronger every day."

Reece put the notebook on her lap. "I'm sorry, Rob. I know it's hard. We're here to hang with you." She tossed the notebook aside. "I was thinking about when divorce happened to me, about what I needed most. More than anything, I just wanted someone my age who understood."

"Wow, same here," I said, remembering my horrible time. "People give you advice. It's usually bad advice, so they feel stupid and disappear. Or they try to act like it's no big deal, and you want to punch them in the face." I leaned back and huffed. "I wanted people to show up and shut up."

"Someday soon we have to make a pact, like Elijah suggested before," Reece said, her voice strong. "A ceremony and some words to say together. For Rob." She bumped Rob's knee with hers and grinned at him, "I have to say you look great, even with what you're going through. You'll have to tell Mei and me all about your week at the beach."

I chuckled low, like Dad. "Guys, when it gets completely dark, let's tell the girls *a certain ghost story.* You can do the honors, Rob. You're the dramatic one."

"Ghost story?" Mei asked.

Reece pulled us back to the subject, "Okay, but later. Got the Quella? Let's think about the threes. Maybe Elijah's name is in the Bible three times."

I punched in the name. "Try a hundred."

"My name's in there a hundred times!?" he practically yelled.

"It means 'God is Yah,' or 'my God is God himself.'"

He was stunned. "My name means 'my God is God himself'?"

"In Hebrew, yeah." I kicked at his foot. "In Indian your name means, 'skinny tree hugger who runs with big feet.' Don't flatter yourself, Navajo. The Bible verses are about the prophet Elijah, not you."

"Read some," he said. "There may be a clue."

"Okay, let's go for Old Testament at the very end. Hold on . . . here it is. 'See, I will send you the prophet Elijah before that great and dreadful day of the LORD comes.'"

"What's that mean?" he asked me.

"That's a Stallard question. But . . . I can tell you one thing: *this* verse isn't about the prophet. He was gone by the time this book was written. It's about another Elijah."

He glanced worriedly at the dark green sky. "The Stallards said the armor might be connected with the coming Day of Evil. Is that the same as the great and dreadful day?"

We sat there surrounded by mannequins, wondering about the great and dreadful day of the Lord, with Mrs. Bates at our side, her bleach bottle head tipping thoughtfully to the left.

"Robbie!!!" a voice shot up the stairwell.

We jumped. "We're up here, Mom!" Rob called.

We went to the top of the stairs. Mrs. Wingate was draped over the banister, looking at us sideways.

"Kids, there's a tornado watch. I just wonder if you should come down until it passes."

"We'll be fine, Mom. And I want to be called Rob now."

She stuck on a smile, as fake as Mrs. Bates's. "Tell you what, kids. The cake will be out of the oven in twenty minutes. I'll call you down then."

"We'll be done by then anyway," Rob snipped. "This is a private meeting, Mom."

"Thanks, Aunt Grace. I love your cakes," Elijah said politely.

I whispered to Rob, "Hey, lighten up on your mom."

"Tornado?" Mei looked terrified. "A storm like this?" With her finger, she drew a swirl of circles in the air.

Reece nodded. "They say it sounds like a train coming. There's no need to worry."

"Unless it drops down without warning," said Elijah, stuck in Day of Evil mode.

"Don't scare her, Creek." I said. "Let's move closer to the window so we can hear."

Most of the journal info fell into the questions-to-ask-the-Stallards category. One thing was obvious: Dowland had been frantically collecting facts and notes, dates and names and places, samples of alphabets, a few addresses, all jumbled together in a rambling mess. He'd scrawled *What?!* or *Why?!* or *When?!* and underlined them several times, big questions on each page with no answers.

"He was collecting research," Rob said.

Reece added, "And he was looking for a connection."

"Connections between what?" Mei asked.

Rob answered, "The armor and history, the armor and

his sermons, or his family, or the number three . . . or Elijah."

I offered to call the Stallards and set up an appointment.

Downstairs in the dining room over big squares of warm lemon cake, we got onto the subject of what our names meant. Reece told Mrs. Wingate, "Elijah's means 'God is God himself.' Mei's name means 'living sprout' in Japanese symbols."

Mrs. Wingate proudly told us that *Robert* meant "bright, shining fame." We gave him grief.

Mei was deciding what the Japanese symbols for each of our names might mean, when the phone rang. Mrs. Wingate picked it up. "Hello?" She gasped, "Where? Thanks!" and slammed down the phone, whirling toward us. "Get to the basement! A tornado has touched down this side of Whitcomb! Let's go!"

Elijah and Mei went for Reece to help her through the kitchen to the basement door. Storm sirens started wailing. Whitcomb was in the next county, four miles to the southwest—too close for comfort.

Halfway to the door Elijah stopped. "The journals! The belt! They're in the tower!"

"You're not going up there!" Rob screamed.

Elijah didn't wait to argue. He was a blur across the kitchen, then gone.

"Elijah, no!" Mrs. Wingate started to go after him.

"Let's head on down," I said, holding the door open.

"We don't want to get in his way when he comes."

Mrs. Wingate asked, "Do you hear something?"

We strained to listen over the sirens. I stepped out on the back stoop for a quick peek at the sky. The clouds were smoky and ragged.

"What is *that* sound?" Mei looked up at me, her dark eyes wide, questioning my face as I listened.

Rob came back up the steps and listened at the door.

"Let's get downstairs, kids. Come on, get inside!" said Mrs. Wingate.

Out of nowhere, a gust of wind blasted the house.

"Inside!" Mrs. Wingate yelled. "Downstairs, everybody! Robbie, where are you going?!"

He ran to the entry hall. "Elijah!?"

"I'll get him!" his mom ordered, and ran past him.

He started after her. "No, Mom! Don't go!"

Mei slammed the back door. "Everyone, come on!"

Every window in the house started whistling.

"Elijah!" Reece screamed, clutching the door casing, refusing to go down.

"Hurry, Reece!" Mei said.

Everyone was yelling, and suddenly there was a blue flash, a loud pop, and the lights went out.

Mass confusion. I ran into someone in the entry hall and bellowed up the stairs, "Creek! It's here! Get down now!!"

From the dark living room came the sound of shattering glass—one window, then another. A gust of cold air hit me. The house trembled; it was coming apart at the seams. Someone screamed. I grabbed the banister. "Creek, NOW!"

Elijah came barreling down the steps, a shadow with a stack of notebooks clutched in one arm, the other arm holding the belt. His feet hardly touched the ground. For an instant it seemed he was airborne. A terrible thought flashed through my mind: that the tornado was on us, and he was being pulled into the vortex.

But down he came and hit the floor running. We tore through the hall and kitchen and hurled ourselves blindly down the basement steps, slamming the door behind us. The house rattled. The girls shrieked for us to get to the corner.

"Where's Mom?!" Rob yelled.

"She came down ahead of us," I yelled back.

"No, she didn't!" he screamed. In the chaos, his mom got left upstairs. Rob tore out for the stairs. "MOM!"

I grabbed his arm. "You can't go up there!" But he ripped himself from my grip and hurtled up the wooden steps.

The girls screamed for him, but he had already thrown himself at the door with a vengeance, breaking it open. My ears popped and the sound went muddy. A hiss was inside my head now. I lunged for the others, threw my arms around them. I felt arms around me. We crushed ourselves into the corner, waiting for the worst. I prayed and held on.

# Chapter 21

**THEN** it was over.

Reece and Mei were in the circle of my arms. Elijah was beside me, to my right, part of the human knot.

"It passed," he said.

I heard him dumping the notebooks on the floor. "Let's go. We've got to find them." The click of metal told me he was putting on the belt.

We picked our way upstairs, testing each creaking step. Lying on the darkened kitchen floor were shards of broken glass. The gleaming shapes crackled as we walked. The walls and ceiling were still there, but stuff was tossed everywhere: dishes, curtains, papers, chairs. . . .

Elijah called out, "Rob? . . . Robbie? Aunt Grace?"

For a moment there was dead quiet, then . . .

"Mom? . . ." Rob was on the floor in the entry hall, his arms wrapped around the banister post. The front door had been blown off. Elijah and I joined him.

"You okay?" I asked.

"Mom?" Rob called out the door.

We got a first glimpse of the damage outside. Before us lay snapped tree limbs, a caved-in roof across the street, and junk scattered all over the yard.

"Oh, man," I said, my voice reverent and awed.

We took a step outside into the dark. The porch furniture was gone. A smashed bike lay in the bushes, and just beyond the steps of the porch, crushed under a big ripped-down tree limb, was a woman's body.

Rob's hollow, broken voice echoed, "Ma! . . ." He walked robotlike to the edge of the porch, his eyes fixed on the dark, still shape.

"Rob, don't!" I said. But he'd dragged himself down the steps before I could make myself reach out to stop him. I felt sick.

He stumbled across the yard and dropped on his knees beside the still form crushed under the limb of the raven's tree. Elijah and I stood shoulder to shoulder in the doorway. My normally brave camp counselor friend had no words of comfort. Neither did I.

We heard a soft moan. Robbie touched the body with a trembling hand.

But the moan wasn't coming from the yard. It was coming from the wall beside us. Elijah spun toward the door of the hall powder room. He yanked it open. Mrs. Wingate stumbled out into the hall. "Robbie? Are you kids okay? I got knocked in there and the pressure on the door . . . I couldn't get it—where's Robbie?"

Elijah ran to the porch. "Your mom's okay! She hid in the bathroom."

Rob's sad, stooped silhouette looked up. "Huh?"

"I think . . . I accidentally pushed her," I said to myself.

"Who—" Rob, a confused shadow, turned jerkily to the body beside him on the ground.

Squinting into the darkness, Elijah started to chuckle. "The dress . . ."

"What?" I asked.

He called, "Rob, don't try to resuscitate Mrs. Bates."

"Mrs. Bates!?" I said in disbelief.

Rob stood and staggered toward us like a drunk.

Mrs. Wingate rushed out to the porch and cried, "Robbie, how did you get out there? Are you all right? Is everyone all right?"

They ran to each other and hugged for a long time.

I followed Elijah out to where the body lay, hoping he knew what he was talking about. I reached down, put my hand on her back, just in case he was wrong. There lay ol' Bleachbottle Bates, looking a little worse for wear. She'd been sucked out of the attic window.

I was so relieved it wasn't Rob's mom, so pumped that all of us were alive and well, I got stupid. "We owe her a funeral," I said, faking sadness.

Elijah put a hand over his heart. "It's the least we can do."

When the girls came out to the porch, they must have thought we'd gone stark raving mad, laughing and yanking at Mrs. Bates until she came out from under the limb in pieces. We kicked her and her stuffing clear out to the curb, preaching in Gullah about the old woman's liftoff.

Mrs. Wingate had more candles than the Vatican. The

kitchen and living room being blown out like they were, we gathered in the dining room, which had somehow stayed intact. She lit the room while the rest of us wandered inside and out to assess the damage to The Castle and to Magdeline at large. Power was out over most of the town. Elijah wanted to run home to check on his family, but his Aunt Grace said, "No, no. There could be wires down; it's too dangerous. Your parents know you're here. They'll come for you when it's safe." Before Elijah could argue, she added, "And I'm sure they're all right. They have a sturdy house and a good basement."

I detected a tone of resentment.

Before long, people were walking the streets with flashlights, checking on their neighbors, cussing over damaged cars, calling for their dogs. Kerosene lanterns appeared on porches. One by one, windows glowed across town. You could hear trees cracking and falling. It was Halloween in April. If a parade of freaks and monsters had come marching down the street, they'd have fit right in.

Mei's terrified parents were the first to arrive. Mrs. Aizawa fluttered over her daughter in Japanese. Mei said to us, "We haven't seen tornadoes in Japan. My mother's a fright."

Reece cackled. "You mean she's frightened."

Mrs. Wingate invited the Aizawas inside and served juice. She apologized that she couldn't make tea. I couldn't figure her. My mom would have been shoveling broken glass after a twister, not trying for a high tea.

Sirens went off again, and the Aizawas thought the storm was coming back. Rob's mom did her best to put them at ease—those were police sirens and fire engines.

When Elijah's dad didn't show after a while, he got really worried. He paced the floor and kept checking the phone to see if the lines had been fixed. He was going stir-crazy, so Mrs. Wingate said he could go home, but not by himself. I offered to go. She gave us a safety lecture—we were getting a lot of those lately—about watching out for downed wires.

"Follow others and do what the authorities tell you," she said. She outfitted us with flashlights and water bottles.

Calm but hanging close to his mom, Rob gladly stayed behind with the others.

I gave him a friendly punch. "You're the man, Wingate."

The two of us set out walking—me with my board strapped to my back and Elijah wearing the belt of truth. We promised Mrs. Wingate we'd latch onto the first adult heading toward camp.

Main Street was blocked. I'd never seen tornado damage firsthand. Pretty unbelievable. The tornado seemed to have picked places at random: one house was in shambles, the one next to it untouched, trucks upside down here, trees snapped like twigs there. We walked in silence, careful of every step.

"What a mess," Elijah said.

"One minute, two minutes tops—that's all it took."

"Things can change so fast," he said in wonder.

We worked our way through the business district, which had suffered some major damage. People milled around, stunned.

"I hope everyone's okay," he said after a while.

We picked up the pace. "I wish I could use my board."

"Too dangerous. You might hit a wire. I wish we could see the exact path of the tornado."

I pointed my flashlight to the flat, third-floor roof of a real estate office. "Up there you'd get a view of the damage."

He hesitated.

"It'll only take a minute. Bird's-eye view. I bet you can see camp from there."

We took off down a side alley and stopped where a fire escape zigzagged over our heads toward the night sky. "That'll get you to the roof. I'll give you a boost."

"You can go first," he offered.

I tried to sound casual. "Uh, no, I'm cool down here."

"'Kay," he said, looking at me curiously. He threw a stick at the fire escape to make sure it wasn't electrified from a downed wire.

We clicked off our flashlights. I unhitched the board from my back, entwined my fingers to make a stirrup, and boosted him up. He missed his first grab for the ladder and went hurtling into a bunch of garbage cans, making a terrific clatter. I died laughing. He made it on the second try. Swinging back and forth to get momentum, he flung his leg over the ladder, reached one arm, and swung up to the landing—the big monkey.

"I'll pull you up," he said.

"I'm cool," I answered casually, though my knees got weak at the idea. "Have your look."

"C'mon," he said.

"That's all right. I'll wait for the news photos."

"What are you boys doing?!" came a gruff voice out of the dark.

"Nothing," Elijah answered the voice. "Just heading home, and we wanted to see how the tornado went through the town."

A burly man came out from behind the store with a rifle. My first thought was *Theobald*. A live current ran down my fingers and toes.

"Sir, we got caught in the storm at a friend's house," I said from the shadows. He stepped toward me. I recognized him as the pool hall owner.

"No looting, you hear!" he barked. "I got a gun. Come out where I can see you."

"Yes, sir," I said respectfully and stepped out.

"He's Marcus Skidmore," came the voice from above. "I'm Elijah Creek. My dad runs Camp Mudjokivi. We were down at my aunt's house when the tornado hit. We wanted to see the path of the storm from up high so that we could stay away from any trouble spots."

The man grumbled. "Awright," he drawled, "but not from my building. Get down and keep moving."

Elijah apologized for trespassing. I upstaged him and said it was my idea, that I was sorry too, and hoped none of his properties had suffered damage.

We walked on, taking in the chaos the tornado had caused. The sirens, the echoes of people frantically calling out names, tree branches crackling, the smell of leaking gas and settling dust—it was surreal.

Elijah said, "My dad should have come after me by now."

"Mine too," I said casually, though a dark feeling crept over me. "They probably couldn't get through yet. They could have passed us up, gone another way maybe, a back street or . . ." My voice trailed off unconvincingly.

"If the tornado kept a straight path, it missed both our houses," he said hopefully.

"Yeah." Dark, scary images flickered through my mind. I pushed them away. I couldn't lose my dad again. I wondered if Mom and Dad were together, and if they were looking for me.

# Chapter 22

WE reached the camp and walked into the wide hugs of
Mr. and Mrs. Creek. Little Nori and Stacy, both wide-eyed
and clutching their teddy bears, ran to their big brother
and squeezed his legs. Mr. Creek said Bo had gotten stuck
in traffic coming after Elijah; he'd seen us at a distance
heading toward camp and walkie-talkied them that we
were coming. I asked if they'd mind letting my parents
know where I was.

As it turned out, Mom and Dad and Bo made it to The
Castle and were helping Mrs. Wingate. I pictured Mom
shoveling broken glass, Dad checking for structure damage.
They relayed the message through Bo's walkie-talkie for me
to stay at the camp. It was great to hear their voices. Our
condo was safe, they said, and if there was damage to the
camp grounds, the Creeks would need the extra muscle for
cleanup in the morning. School would be canceled for sure.
Elijah and I weren't crushed over that news.

Some of the power was back on by morning, but school
was still called off. The gas and electric company had
to check the lines, and a damaged corner of the school
building had to be fixed before it was safe.

When I rolled out of bed, Elijah was already up. He and

his dad were on the porch with mugs of hot drink. Elijah turned when he heard me creak open the screen door. "Dad says we can get a good view of town from the hayloft of Morgan's barn if you want."

"Sure," I said without thinking.

"Ever been up there?" Elijah asked.

"I'm not a farm-type person."

Mr. Creek said, "You haven't lived until you've built a hay fort or had a rotten egg explode in your face." He gazed out over the grounds and heaved a sigh of relief. "The camp looks good from here. We escaped most of the damage, but those trails may need to be cleared. After you've checked out the woods, you boys can go to Morgan's. Be careful. That loft is higher than it looks."

I laughed it off with a lump in my chest.

Elijah and I took a golf cart with a utility wagon hitched on the back into Owl Woods to gather up debris. The funnel cloud hadn't touched down anywhere on the camp, but there were lots of broken branches. We cleared the ones across the path, and cleaned up random junk that had blown in from other parts of town: books, papers, clothes, hunks of metal. . . .

Hurling stuff into the wagon, I said, "You know, Creek, if the tornado had come a little closer to Rob's house, or if you had been a few seconds later, Dowland's secrets, the belt of truth, and some of your body parts would have been sucked out of the tower, just like Mrs. Bates, and scattered all over town. A few seconds and a few feet difference, this could be pieces of you I'm picking up."

He said, "I thought of that," and kept working.

Mr. Morgan waved at us from his back porch as we crossed his meadow. He gave us the okay sign. The barn had a pretty cool hay smell. We climbed ladders to the upper hayloft, an enormous platform, empty and spreading across the whole top of the barn.

"There's no hay," I said.

"They've used it up feeding livestock over the winter," Elijah said. "There's the view—up there." He nodded to a high open window casting a shaft of bright dusty light on the floor. A pulley dangled in front of it.

"How are we supposed to—" I started to ask.

"We'll use the pulley and rope," he said.

"Sure, okay," I said, though this farm stuff wasn't my area.

"I'll haul *you* up first this time," he said, not making eye contact.

By now—after the palm tree incident and the fire escape incident—he'd picked up on my uncertainty about heights, but he was too cool to rub it in.

He made a loop for my foot, I grabbed the rope. He pulled the other end over his shoulder, turned, leaned in with his whole weight, and started walking toward the back of the loft. Up I went, lurching higher with every heave-ho, until my sight line cleared the bottom of the window. The view was seriously cool. I was above every rooftop, eye level with the only church steeple in town. I muttered in astonishment, "Whoa."

He stopped.

"I'm not all the way up yet," I said.

"You yelled whoa!" he said, his voice straining from the haul.

"I meant it's a great view. A few more feet and I can sit on the window. I'll cut the horse talk."

He laughed and grunted. "Horses don't talk, Skid."

"I meant—" He lurched me up again, I grabbed the edge of the opening. My head swam.

"Are you on?" he grunted.

I hung my backside on the edge of the window. "Don't let go yet. There's no place to hang onto, no fingerhold." My throat went dry. I reached behind me, grabbed onto the frame of the window as best I could, slung one leg out, and clamped myself to the wall with my feet, like a clothespin. "Okay. I'm up." I looked out across Morgan's farm and thought, *I'm waaay up.*

"I hope you don't have hay fever. One good sneeze and you're gone," Elijah joked.

Sweat popped out on my forehead. "Not funny," I said.

"Anchor your end of the rope, so I can pull myself up."

I couldn't move. "To what?"

"Anything but yourself," he said dryly.

I felt around, turned my head cautiously. "There's nothing. Not even a nail."

"Okay, then take your foot out of the rope."

It was hard to breathe, much less move. I couldn't make my foot unclamp to shake the rope free. It was a fifteen-foot fall to the loft on one side, a forty-foot drop to hard ground on the other. One way meant a few broken bones, the other was death.

I fought panic as I looked down at Elijah.

"You're afraid of heights," he said with a grin.

I blew air out. "Didn't used to be," I answered shakily.

Elijah let down the loop, stuck his foot in, and pulled himself up. He plopped down on the window. The wall trembled, and I made a sound.

"We can't let this go," he said, wrapping his fingers around the rope, "or we'll be good and stuck up here. Take it easy. If you start to fall, I'll grab you."

If there was one person in the world I'd let see me in my not-so-cool times, it would be Elijah Creek. He'd never ambush an innocent guy.

Scary or not, the view was awesome. I made myself enjoy it. The tornado had taken a southwest to northeast swipe across the middle of town, bouncing over some buildings, smashing others like a big fist would.

"Looks like it was a narrow one," Elijah said. "Some tornadoes can leave a path a half mile wide."

"Whoa . . . there'd have been no town left!"

I breathed easier after a while, but he brought it up again. "So that explains why you wouldn't go up the tree with Rob at the beach, why you didn't want to go up on the building last night. Fear of heights."

"It's weird," I shrugged. "It came all of a sudden."

"What changed?"

"I don't know, man." I thought on it a long time. "That thing with Salem, I guess. You understand what I'm saying? Stuck out in the open, no weapon, nowhere to run. Nothing like that had ever happened to me. I never thought I could die so . . . you know, easy."

"I know. Same here."

We sat there knee to knee, straddling the barn loft window high above Magdeline. I glanced over at him. He was studying the town on some deep level. There was something mysterious about Elijah; I always knew it. Something good, a certain power in his quiet ways. People like the Brill Brothers gave him a hard time because his kind of strength they knew nothing about, and it bugged them.

"Everything's changed," he said eerily.

"Mostly through the center of town," I laughed.

He shook his head, eyes still on the horizon. "I don't mean that."

"I know. But . . . what *do* you mean?"

He looked at me with a dark, wild, scared look. "Signs. The raven, the wave, the storm. They were signs . . . for us."

"Bad things happen," I shrugged. "You've grown up

in this little town, sheltered from the cold, cruel world out there." I was trying to keep things light. "Maybe it's just the barometric pressure. It affects the weather, bird behavior, our moods," I said, quoting Mr. Saylor in science class. I slipped the Quella out of my pocket. "So let's be scientific about this; ix-nay on the superstitions."

I punched in *raven* and scrolled through the references. "Okay, Noah sent a raven from the ark. When it didn't come back, that was a sign the flood waters had receded."

He shook his head. "It's piling up. Finding the armor, the church burning, Salem's attacks, discovering those bodies, Rob's accident. They are all messages."

"In the Bible," I went on, "it says ravens were not to be eaten, that God feeds the ravens when they call. Oh, and here's something cool . . . another Elijah verse. God ordered ravens to feed Elijah. God told him, 'You will drink from the brook, and I have ordered the ravens to feed you there.'"

"Let me see that," he practically grabbed it out of my hand, and read on, "'The ravens brought him bread and meat in the morning and bread and meat in the evening.'"

I said, "See there, the raven was a good sign. Think about it, Rob's parents were already having problems when the raven showed up, weren't they?"

"I guess . . ."

"When it showed up at the church and toppled the beams, you weren't hurt and neither was Reece. As for the wave, it actually rolled Rob back to shore, overpowering the undertow. If the wave hadn't come, he might have gone out too far and been swept away by smaller waves."

"Maybe."

I looked over the town. "The tornado? So okay, the town's a mess. We *might* find some good in it. The wind and the waves obey God. It's in the Book."

I was halfway enjoying myself up there, feeling smart for coming up with these ideas, putting everything together in a package. I said after a long while, "Something has changed, though: us. We're changing."

Elijah straddled the barn wall as easily as sitting on the arm of a chair. He was fearless of the height, probably from spending so much time up in Great Oak. His eyes moved across the town with the focus of a warrior. What he was looking for, he couldn't find, and it bothered him.

"You know," he said worriedly, "Uncle Dorian's supposed to be staying at The Roanoke. Mom told me."

"Yeah?"

He nodded to the east end of town. "It should be there. But . . . it's not. The old hotel isn't there anymore."

# Chapter 23

WE sprinted across Morgan's field back to camp and burst into the maintenance building. "Need anything from uptown, Dad? Skid and I are going to see the damage."

Mr. Creek looked up from his clipboard. He was doing inventory on the shelves. "I think we're going to need to rent another chainsaw to cut up those fallen branches. That's one advantage of the storm—we need the firewood."

I nodded to Elijah. "See, a good thing already."

Mr. Creek rubbed his eyes like he was really tired. "Don't get in the way of any cleanup crews. And watch out for—"

"Electric lines and falling buildings. We're on it," finished Elijah. "Um, Dad, where's Uncle Dorian?"

Mr. Creek's words came fast and flat. "Don't know, son, but I'm sure he's fine."

I dodged trash cans, limbs, and hunks of house debris, stopping to carry my skateboard over the big stuff. Elijah hurdled over the junk and made better time. I caught up with him at The Roanoke.

One whole side of the old brick hotel was gone. It was weird how one exposed room had all the furniture sucked out of it, but a plastic shower curtain still hung around a bathtub. Townspeople had gathered, all commenting about the fickle ways of a tornado. Some were asking about missing people. We were wondering out loud if Rob had seen the hotel yet when he walked up by himself.

"Hey," we said.

"Hey," he said back, looking at the damage.

"What's up?" I asked.

"Nothing."

"How's your house?" Elijah asked.

"Some windows are blown out, roof tiles off, some stuff missing." He shoved his hands in his pockets.

"Where's your dad?" Elijah blurted out.

Rob's lip started to quiver. He looked up at the shower curtain blowing in the breeze. "A couple days ago he was here."

We stared at the ripped-open hotel and didn't say anything for a minute.

Elijah asked gently, "Hasn't he called?"

Rob shook his head.

"He will," Elijah said.

Rob wandered off without saying a word. Elijah started to follow.

I said, "Let him be. We'll go over there later and start work on his house."

We wandered the street. Over the first shock, people were gearing up for cleanup and rebuilding.

A man hurried past, rolling up his shirt sleeves. "You boys doing anything?"

"I have to rent a chainsaw for my dad," Elijah answered.

"Get in line," he said with a sour smile. "They've all been sold, rented, or borrowed in two counties. We're putting together volunteer cleanup crews. You have a few hours?"

Before we could answer, he steered us into the real estate office where a map of Magdeline was fastened to the wall. Someone had drawn a wide band across the town at an angle and colored it in with a red marker—the path of destruction.

"We're taking sign-ups at that table," he said in an irritated tone. "Sure could use your help. You missed the free pizza—pay for a morning's work—but they're bringing dinner in if you work all afternoon. Pick up an ID badge and gloves; trash bags and shovels are behind the building. Somebody back there will set you up. If nobody's there, come back this way. We're still getting organized. Dinner's served out of Florence's at 6:00, while it lasts. By the way, you need to be caught up on your tetanus shots—lots of dirty, rusty stuff around. Let your parents know where you are."

He was called away, and we studied the map, pointing out familiar places that had been hit. Suddenly Elijah nudged me and nodded to the map. "High Street," he whispered. "Theobald's."

"What?"

A grin spread across his face. "Don't you get it? They need people to volunteer—I don't believe this—we can go over to Theobald's with gloves and bags and shovels! It couldn't get any easier than this."

I couldn't believe it either. "Safe passage in broad daylight? And get this! With the cleanup, Theobald will be on his dozer around the clock for the next month! This is good stuff!"

Elijah's smile faded. He gazed at the red path of destruction across the map with something like fear in his eyes. The twister had passed through town, nicked The Castle, spared the rest of our houses, and given us access to Theobald's forbidden property to search for the armor of God. I knew what Elijah was thinking: *someone you can't see is helping you.*


We called home for permission to be on the cleanup brigade and ran to the High Street bridge over the railroad, the best vantage point for viewing Theobald's house. Crates and clothes and furniture were strewn everywhere. A run-down car in his yard was wearing a mashed-up riding mower on its roof. A lawn chair hung in the tree, and there was some damage to the roof and siding. The tornado had dumped debris on the tracks below his house, and there was already a crew on the job. Elijah pointed out Theobald down by the tracks, at the wheel of his dozer, grizzly and sweaty and looking seriously ticked off. The picture wasn't as rosy as we'd hoped. We watched the railroad crew from the bridge.

"He knows me," Elijah warned.

"Let's get off here in case he looks up," I said. "We'll circle around to the other side of the house, check out our options."

"We're looking for fresh dirt," Elijah reminded me as we went, "a place big enough for Dowland to bury a piece of armor this size." He spread his hands a foot apart. "A hidden place, maybe covered with leaves or behind a shed."

We passed the front of the house, picking up bits of garbage in the yard. I followed Elijah's lead. He made a sharp left around to the side of the house hidden from the tracks. We opened the bags and dropped in garbage as we found it, our eyes racing over the property.

"Hey, boys!" A slim, middle-aged woman in jeans and T-shirt approached. "You're needed down on the tracks. We have trains wanting to come through. You can get this later."

"Sure," I said.

She headed around the house. I glanced at Elijah. "I don't know, Creek. Going down there right under his nose? It's pretty—"

"We'll take the risk." He riffled in his garbage bag and pulled out an old ball cap. He put it on. "Does this help?"

"You still look like you. How good a look did he get before?"

He pulled the bill down further. "Let's take our time getting down to the tracks. Better yet, let's split up. You circle back around the front. I'll take the back. Sweep the hill, meet at the bottom."

There was a gleam in Elijah's visor-shaded eyes when we met at the bottom. "I found a place!" he yelled over the roar of the dozer.

"Yeah?" I yelled back. "Where?"

I followed his eyes up the hill. "See those old rosebushes?"

At the back corner of the property was a bramble of long thorny, arched branches.

"Under there," he said. "There's a pile of fresh dirt under the thorns."

# Chapter 24

fOR the next couple of hours, Elijah wore the ball cap
and stayed downwind of Bruce Theobald while we flung a
few hundred pounds of trash off the tracks. I hung close to
the work crew and overheard Theobald's plans to let the
city use his dozer while he concentrated on fixing his roof.

With that piece of info, we went back into town,
gathering junk on the way. The rest of the afternoon we
hauled salvage to Lost and Found at the Tesslers' three-
car garage, where people could look for important stuff
that had blown out of their houses. We cashed in on the
free dinner of barbecue, baked beans, and chips, and then
headed back to camp.

Elijah called the others with the good news (that we may
have found the site of the buried armor) and the bad news
(it was under a thornbush at Theobald's place, on a bank
overlooking the tracks and the backside of town). Hidden
in plain sight, but off-limits any way you slice it.

The Creeks had heard from Rob's dad; he'd been safe
in Columbus when the storm hit. He said he'd be back in
town soon. I passed the news along to Mei, then to Reece,
who almost cried from relief. I felt strangely dark and
moody. Sure, I was happy the horrible time didn't have my
name on it, but now I was raging against Dorian Wingate

for his kid's sake. Funny how someone you hardly know can pass along so much damaging crud—like second-hand cigarette smoke.

That night another whirlwind began, a whirlwind of the Stallard variety. I called them about our needing help with the journals and about the possible location of the breastplate of righteousness. Dr. Eloise took off with gale force: "Tremennnndous! We must get together ASAP! You didn't happen to get Mr. Dowland's address book along with the journals, did you? No? Well, not to worry. I'm ahead of myself. Dale will be elated with this progress report. Let's see, let's see, we simply can't get away from our duties here at present. But oh, this is wonnnnderful. Might you children arrange a flight or rail passage to Chicago? We'll pay your expenses, of course, but consult your parents; we wouldn't want another snafu."

I called the others, who talked to their parents, who called my parents, who talked it over with me again. Then another round of calls later that night. By strange coincidence, or divine plan, Reece's mom was back from Pittsburgh and had upcoming business just outside of Chicago.

Reece got on the phone. "Mom can't believe the Stallards would pay her way up. She'll love having us for company. She hates those long, lonely drives."

It was day clean. Mrs. Elliston picked us all up, getting Rob last so she could say a few words to his mom while we crammed the luggage in. By this time Rob's house looked seriously haunted. The windows in the living room and the tower were boarded up. Broken tree limbs covered the yard. Mrs. Bates's bald head smiled at passersby from the gutter. The For Sale sign, which had blown away, was back in the yard with another sign attached to the top: Price Reduced.

Rob came out to the car glassy-eyed, acting spaced. "Another road trip . . ."

"Party while you can," I said and got in next to Reece.

As we pulled out to the street, I realized something. "See that limb that snapped off and killed Mrs. Bates? It was the raven's perch just a few weeks before. Hey, Creek," I said mysteriously, "it could be a sign of things to come . . . Mrs. Bates plus raven equals boo hag!"

"It's a sign all right—a sign you're a jerk," Elijah joked, knocking me in the back of the head.

"What do you mean, a sign?" Mei asked. "I'm learning road signs so I can get my driver's license."

Reece said, "Elijah is looking for direction from God."

"I am?" he asked.

"Yes, you are," Reece said. "We're not blind."

"Word of caution, kids," Mrs. Elliston said. "Signs from God must be read very carefully. That's a big responsibility. You must check everything with Scripture. If it doesn't agree with the Word, it's not from God." She paused.

"What kinds of signs have you seen or heard, Elijah?"

He looked embarrassed. "I don't know."

"Yes, you do!" Reece said.

"Well . . . I heard the answer 'signs' in my head."

"What was the question?" I asked.

"I said we needed help finding the other pieces of the armor."

We sang camp songs, played the alphabet game, and helped Mei with road signs. This trip didn't have the macho mood of the Farr Island trip, but I couldn't have cared less. Leaving the ruins of Magdeline suited me fine. By noon we were seeing skyscrapers in the distance. After the last pit stop, we switched seats. Rob the map king and Mei rode shotgun, navigating us off the interstate and into downtown traffic. We had a run-in with a taxi driver, but Mrs. Elliston just smiled and waved.

She dropped us off down a seedy Chicago side street. Looking worried, she said, "This is the address, I'm sure . . . so . . . I guess you should go on in. Their office is on the twelfth floor. I'll park the car in the first spot I find and be right back. Stay together."

We rode up on a cracker box elevator, the kind with a window in the door where you can see the walls dropping as you go up. At the end of a dark, narrow hall, on an old-fashioned, ripple-glassed door were words printed in black and gold: Antiquities Research Center.

"Here it is." I tried the knob. "It's open."

Just inside the door, a wooden crate the size of a small coffin was stretched between two chairs. It was torn open, packing straw yanked out and flung all over the carpet. Piles of manila folders were dumped on file cabinets and shelves; books were thrown open.

*Ransacked!* I thought. *A robber looking for stash; he might still be here!* I put my arm out to hold the others back. "Shh!"

A second look told me the Stallards' office wasn't ransacked, just junked—with books and boxes, carousel trays of slides, and science magazines. Two huge side-by-side desks faced us in front of the windows. There was no seeing the top of anything, or finding a place to stand. You got the idea the Stallards were in the middle of a hundred projects marked *Rush!*

Rob went right to a cracked glass display case and wowed over the ancient pottery and bones. Packing straw crunched under his shoes.

Reece gasped. "What happened here?"

Elijah peeked into the empty crate and muttered, "Looks like *The Curse of the Mummy's Tomb.*"

"Research!" answered a crackly voice from behind all that manila. Then a gasp and, "You're alive!"

Elijah and I went between the desks and peeked over the piles. Wearing gray slacks, a white shirt with rolled up sleeves, and green suspenders, Dr. Dale was propped against the wall, his books spread out on the only open spot left: the floor in front of the window. He motioned us in. I thought that remark about being alive was for our surviving the trip, until I saw the phone at his ear. He raised a finger for us to wait until he finished. "To fight another day," he said enthusiastically to the person on the line. "Yes, of course, come on up! Tell Blessing that when he gets those Ugaritic texts deciphered, I'd love a copy."

He hung up the phone. "Welcome, welcome," he said to us, forcing his creaky bones to stand. "Come in and have a—" he looked around. "Well, give me a minute here." He spun in a circle looking for available chairs that everyone knew weren't there. "Better yet, let's go to the conference room where we can talk." We turned to leave. "But wait! Eloise will be here presently. Yes, I should do a little reorganizing." He started shuffling folders.

Rob whispered to me, "Get comfortable. I'd say we have six months."

"You've gotten humorous lately," I said. "Good to see you're coming around."

"I'm tan now, that's why," he said.

The narrow office was lined with artifacts and replicas of ancient sculptures. Framed parchments in Hebrew, Greek, and hieroglyphics hung on the walls. Stuck on a bulletin board were yellowed articles from foreign newspapers, with old photos of the Stallards standing by holes in the desert or receiving awards at banquets.

We were occupying ourselves, nosing around the

bookshelves, when in came what looked like a sand volleyball player: medium height, strong and trim, shaved head, white shirt, tan shorts, and flip-flops. The guy was surprised to see us. His clear blue eyes crinkled when he smiled. Dr. Stallard dropped an armload of paperwork, threw his scrawny arms around him for a second, then pulled back with a jerk, his forehead knotted with worry.

"Where is . . . she?"

"She's safe," he said with a smile. "Still there."

I figured this was the guy Dr. Dale had just been talking to on the phone.

He glanced at us. "New students?"

"They're helping me with a project," said Dr. Dale.

"Great. Which one?"

Instead of answering, Dr. Dale introduced us. "Children, I'd like you to meet a good friend of mine—" he blanked for a second, "Donovan." He nodded to me, then to each one of us in turn. "Now, this is Marcus; his parents are in the military. We became friends while in the Middle East. And this is Mei, from Japan."

The man bowed deeply and said, *"Konnichiwa."*

Mei covered her mouth and giggled. "You know Japanese?"

"Not much," he said.

"And this is Reece."

"Nice to meet you."

"Nice to meet you too."

Donovan was the kind of person you took to right away: friendly but not shmoozy.

"And Robbie," Dr. Dale went around the circle.

"He goes by Rob now," I said.

"I see." Dr. Dale looked him over. "Rob. It does seem to suit you now. You've grown, haven't you?"

Rob blushed. "An inch and three-quarters."

Dr. Dale said finally, "And this . . . is Elijah."

A look flickered between the two men. We all saw it.

"Very nice to meet you, Elijah," Donovan said, shaking his hand.

The sound of shoes clicking down the hall sent Dr. Dale rushing to the door. He stuck his head out into the hall. "Eloise! You won't believe it. Look who's here, Eloise. It's Ga—it's Donovan!"

Elijah and I swapped suspicious glances. They weren't using his real name.

Dr. Eloise practically skidded into the office, dropped her bag, and gave him a big squeeze. "When we didn't hear, we . . . well, it's so good to see you—ah!" She whirled around. "Did you come by yourself?"

"Yes, but we're all fine."

"Wonderful. And you've met the children?" she asked.

"Yes, the professor says they're helping you with a project."

"Oh, they're little pros, they are. We couldn't have asked for a better team."

Dr. Dale handed Donovan a stack of folders and

something in a paper sack. "This is all the information I have at this time. More forthcoming. Where are you staying, and for how long?"

Serious vibes passed between them, like I've seen in talks my parents used to have right before one of them left on a mission.

"At the Hudson," said the man known as Donovan. "I'm not sure how long. I may have some down time." He turned to us. "It was good to meet you all of you. I'd like to sit and talk sometime."

As soon as he left, I asked the Stallards, "Hey, a couple of questions. What was in that crate?"

"Ah," said Dr. Dale, patting the packing straw, "our terra-cotta Babylonian demon head, seventh century B.C. It's being tested for authenticity."

"Cool. And next question: Donovan—that's not his real name, is it?"

Dr. Eloise's eyebrows went up. First she looked like she was going to say yes. Then she paused. "No. No, it isn't."

We waited for an explanation.

She pressed her hands together, smiling. "Let's go to the conference room and have some tea, why don't we?"

# Chapter 25

✳✳✳✳✳✳✳✳✳✳✳✳✳✳✳✳✳✳✳✳✳✳✳✳✳✳✳✳✳✳✳✳✳✳✳✳✳✳✳✳✳✳✳✳✳✳✳✳

REECE'S mom met up with us in the hall. She had an hour on the parking meter. The conference room was clean and modern, nothing like the office. We gathered around a big wooden table as if we were having a company board meeting. Dr. Eloise served sandwiches and baklava, tea and coffee, and said, "Children, your stay here won't all be boring and stuffy, just talking of journals. We will have fun too."

Rob leaned over to me. "After tea we get to take afternoon naps."

"Yeah, you're real humorous now," I whispered back.

"Let me explain about Donovan," said Dr. Dale. "He and his wife are working in The Window, an extremely dangerous area of the world. He goes by an alias for his protection."

"He's a spy?" Rob asked.

Dr. Dale smiled. "Not a spy."

Casually I mentioned, "I met a couple of spies, because of my dad's work."

"Oh, really?" asked Dr. Eloise.

"I was little at the time. But I caught on to the conversation."

Reece rolled her eyes at me. "Secret agent in training pants."

I tossed a corner of my sandwich across the table at her.

"All I'm saying is they don't live in the shadows and talk in code like, 'The crow flies east on Wednesday.'"

"Nobody thinks that anymore," Reece snipped.

Rob faked a worried look. "You mean crows *don't* fly east on Wednesday?!"

Everybody was getting funny on me.

"Spies are just like the rest of us, that's all I'm saying."

"The Window?" Reece asked, pulling us back on course. "What's that?"

"It's called The Window, but it's not an open window. It's nearly closed," Dr. Eloise said sadly.

"If Donovan's not a spy, what *is* he?" Rob asked.

Dr. Eloise perked up. "Good question, but why don't *you* tell *me?* Let's have a riddle: He goes where he's not wanted. He . . . he tells people what they don't want to hear. He—" she turned to her husband, "help me out, dear."

Dr. Dale continued, "He works with governments while working against them, but all for their ultimate good. He spreads secrets of global importance, and if he's captured or killed, no one will be held accountable."

"Double agent!" said Rob.

When Reece's mom smiled I had a hint.

Reece asked, "Donovan's a missionary?"

The Stallards smiled, "Good girl! Excellent!"

Mei asked, "Missionary?"

"They go all over the world telling people about God," Reece explained.

"Many, many missionaries are risking their lives as we speak," Dr. Eloise said soberly.

Elijah looked skeptical. "Sounds like high level national security."

Dr. Dale said, "The highest level! Where Donovan is— in The Window—there are places that, if you're caught, your chance of survival is—"

Dr. Eloise broke in, "—is not good. And for the record, he doesn't get paid to do what he does. He gets paid to do something else."

"I don't understand!" Mei said. I was confused myself.

"He works at a regular job that allows him to do the dangerous work on the side," said Dr. Eloise. "Quite a riddle, isn't it?"

Dr. Dale leaned back, thoughtfully. "Over the centuries, an estimated thirty to fifty million people have been executed for doing what he does: living their faith in hostile territory. Over two hundred million are being threatened or persecuted even as we speak."

Across the table, Elijah had pulled out of the discussion. With his thumb and middle finger he rotated his cup, watching it go around and around, not saying a word.

"Okay, what's Donovan's real name?" I asked Dr. Dale jokingly. "Come on, we won't tell."

Dr. Dale laced his fingers together on the table. He pressed his lips so tight they disappeared. "I'm sorry, son. We can't do that."

"But he knows about us," Rob argued. "He knows our names."

"Why is it dangerous?" Mei asked.

Dr. Eloise passed the teapot around. "He's fighting the war to end all wars." She started clearing the plates.

Mrs. Elliston looked at her watch. "Sorry to rush off. I need to be in Wheaton in an hour."

Dr. Dale stood. "Then you should be on your way."

Mrs. Elliston hugged everyone and made plans with the Stallards to meet for late dinner.

When the door closed, Dr. Dale said, "Let's get down to business. Tell us about your problem."

Elijah came out of his zone. "We think we know where the next piece is, but we can't get to it."

"Where is it?"

Reece answered, "Behind Theobald's house. He was Dowland's daughter's boyfriend, remember? He's the last one who knows what really happened to her."

"I see, I see," said Dr. Dale, taking notes. "How did you find its location in the first place? We're interested in your deductive processes."

I spoke up. "Elijah and I think Dowland buried things in their opposite environments."

"How so?" Dr. Dale asked.

"The helmet of salvation was outside an old, dead church where no one is saved anymore. The belt of truth, buried with a compass, pointed us to the town's old lies."

"So," Dr. Dale baited us, "the breastplate of righteousness would be in . . ."

"An unrighteous place," Elijah said. "Or what Dowland thought was the most evil place."

Dr. Dale nodded. "I see. The home of his enemy. Brilliant." He glanced at his wife.

"Stunning. They'll keep us on our toes, no doubt," she said, looking a bit uneasy. "And why can't you retrieve it?"

Rob summed it up: "Theobald is big and mean, and he hates us because we brought the scandal to light, and all fingers are pointing at him now. We can't dig without asking. It's trespassing. And we can't ask him because he's so ticked he might dig it up himself and trash it for spite."

The Stallards looked at each other long and hard.

"What do you think, dear?" he said.

She tapped her fingertips together. "Iffy."

He agreed. "Definitely iffy." He finished writing and put his pen down. "If you children would occupy yourselves awhile . . ."

"Don't you want to see the journal notes?" Reece asked.

"Oh yes! Certainly!"

Reece handed over the notes. "The real journals are stuck at the police station, but I wrote down the things I thought could apply to the armor."

Dr. Eloise glanced up. "The police station."

"Yes," said Reece. "The case still has loose ends and the journals are evidence."

"Can you make out anything?" Elijah asked the professors. "Like what it says about me—what that means?"

The professors frowned over the pages. He'd point to a word, and she'd nod. She'd point to another word, and he'd nod. Then Dr. Dale sat up straight. "Well, this is all quite perplexing. More thought needed, I'm afraid." They had a brief, whispery discussion. Then he said, "If you children would occupy yourselves for a bit, we'd like to research these phrases. We have another class this afternoon, and we'd like to look over these notes as well. Here's money for the El Train and a snack. Here's a map; you are . . . here. There's a wonderful aquarium and a park near the lake. The restaurants around Michigan Avenue are marvelous. If you should happen to get lost, take a cab. Here's our address and phone number again. We'll see you back here by 6:00. This isn't the best neighborhood, but it's a short walk to the main thoroughfare. I should say we've never personally had any trouble. Marcus, you're comfortable guiding the others?"

I stood and spread my hands in grand style. "Come, my people! Let us be shakin'!" *Another day on the loose. Hallelujah!*

As we put our chairs back in place, Dr. Eloise pulled Reece aside, and gestured toward the cane. "What is your . . . situation there?"

"It's called slipped capital femoral epiphysis, or skiffy for short."

Dr. Eloise flipped through her mental files. "I've heard of

it. Rather unusual, but remedied by surgery, isn't it?"

"Mine's not following the textbook. The doctors can't figure it."

"Will you be all right today?"

Reece tipped her head in our direction and grinned. "Yes, ma'am. I've got them."

We headed toward the door of the conference room, Elijah in the lead. He suddenly stopped in the doorway. We jammed like logs behind him.

"Hey, what's the deal?" I complained.

He turned and gave the Stallards the strangest look.

"What is it, dear?" Dr. Eloise said. "Oh, you're worried, aren't you? Such a big city. Well, you'll be just fine. Don't stray farther than you feel comfortable."

"Dale . . . and . . . Eloise," Elijah said mysteriously.

"Yes?" she said curiously.

"Are those . . . *your* real names?"

A look stranger than Elijah's spread across their faces: embarrassment, shock. Then faint smiles. They were impressed with Elijah's quick mind. We knew the answer before they said a word.

"Well actually no, dears, those are not our real names. Now have a nice day. And be back on time. We're taking you to a very special place tonight."

"Why?" Rob asked suspiciously.

"For dinner, of course."

# Chapter 26

NOBODY said a word until we were out of the cracker box elevator and on the street, headed for the main drag.

"What is going on?" Elijah asked. "If they're not spies and not missionaries—"

"So they have fake names," I stayed cool. "They admitted it."

"We *have* to tell Mom when she gets back," Reece said.

Mei spoke up. "She won't come back all day. Should we call our parents?"

"Chill," I said. "They're scientists working in The Window. My dad checked them out, remember? You saw their pictures on the wall. They're global science geniuses. They do weird things."

"Yeah, like lying," Rob smirked.

"They're not lying," I defended. "It's like witness protection. You're thinking they should act normal—or what you *Ohioans* call normal, you know what I mean?"

We headed out toward Michigan Avenue. Elijah got in step beside me. "I still don't get that whole thing."

"The Window? Probably the Middle East or parts of Asia," I said with a shrug.

Rob said, "But they're in Chicago! And why don't they trust us? We're kids, we're no threat."

Reece said kindly, "It's because we're not all believers."

Rob went right on, "Well, I'm not going someplace special with them unless your mom goes too."

"It'll be fine," I said, sauntering along. We got to the corner. I looked back down the narrow street, gloomy as twilight.

"Hey, Wingate, you like labeling places. Name that."

Rob looked back, blinked. "I'd call it East Iffy."

We chilled all afternoon, keeping easy pace with Reece, strolling the Magnificent Mile. Rob went crazy in a map store, and Mei bought postcards to send to Japan. The Stallards gave us plenty of money, so we went for a high-end place near Lake Michigan. I spotted a sidewalk café. "Shall we snack alfresco?" I offered my elbows to Reece and Mei.

I sat between them, pulled their chairs close, and gave Elijah a wicked wink. We guys couldn't believe that ten days ago we were twisting the heads off intercoastal shrimp for Frogmore stew, and now we were eating them out of an iced goblet with cocktail sauce.

I leaned back and looked around. "Yeah . . . slurping up shrimp in the concrete canyons of Chicago. Seriously cool."

"Way seriously!" said Rob. Being away from home again was doing him good.

For a while we forgot our suspicions of the Stallards and enjoyed the perks of being their personal relic hunters.

Next we hit Hancock Tower. Crowding into one of the world's fastest elevators, we shot the ninety-some floors in thirty-nine seconds. We stepped out to the observatory, a room of windows from ceiling to floor. There was nothing but sky spreading out in all directions. *Where's the city?* I asked myself. We headed for the windows, and the tops of the buildings came into view below us. Without warning, a height fright ten times worse than at Morgan's barn came over me. My knees went to rubber. I found the nearest bench and sank down on it. I tried to stand, took a couple of steps, and ended up on all fours.

Rob laughed. "Hey, you're whiter than me, Skidmore!"

I managed a weak, "Good one, Wingate," while I slithered back onto the bench and dropped my head to my knees. My secret was out.

Elijah played camp nurse again. When the others had their fill of the view, they got me down to street level in a semi-upright position.

We did a sightseeing boat tour out on Lake Michigan. The whole time the others razzed me about what other phobias I might be hiding. Was I afraid of water? docks? tickets? turnstiles? deck chairs? You get the idea.

Mei had a fit over the skyline. "It reminds me of cities in Japan like Osaka and Yokohama. Now I'm sick of home!"

"It's *homesick!*" we bellowed. She was a good sport.

By nineteen hundred hours, we and the Stallards and Mrs. Elliston had gathered at East Iffy. A short cab ride later we were back at Hancock Tower. The elevator jettisoned us up to the ninety-fifth floor. I prayed the whole thirty-nine seconds: *God, don't let me pass out. I have a reputation, and it's dying by the minute. Whatever's for dinner, let me keep it down. And if I pass out, let it be for a good long while. I wouldn't mind just lying there, as long as I don't get stepped on. Don't let anyone do mouth-to-mouth on me. Your will be done. Amen.*

The view was amazing, but I sat with my back to the window and imagined we were on the second floor. We ordered from a menu my mom would have approved: big prices, fancy names, big plates, little bitty food.

Dr. Dale said, "We have so much to chat about, but let's first address group dynamics. The wife and I would like to hear about how the five of you interact with one another, what gifts you bring to the group."

Everyone looked at someone else for the answer; we hadn't thought about it.

Dr. Eloise told her husband, "Perhaps a bit too philosophical, dear. We'll get back to it. On to the journal notes."

Dr. Dale went into classroom mode. "Here are our preliminary findings: clearly Mr. Dowland knew many things we don't. It will be very important to have a look at the actual journals. We believe the armor's purpose is to teach you about spiritual warfare, most likely through the stories of its history. We hope to piece together its journey through time, which may be an enormous task. There are sketchy legends, for which we are searching through our archives. Let's start with what we have: sketches of the helmet and arm piece, and . . . where is the belt of truth?"

"In my backpack. I left it at your office," said Elijah.

"Ah, good. We've explained about the buckle, but the odd-shaped metal pieces attached to the belt have us in a bit of a quandary. The tapestries are quite interesting— definitely North African. The designs are of a lion, ox, man, and eagle. They represent the four faces of creatures that make up the living throne of God, a kind of spiritual chariot that carried him in visions through the minds of his prophets. The four beings have also been matched to the four books of good news: Matthew, Mark, Luke, and John. It is fitting that the belt of truth should carry the Word of God in symbols."

He took a drink of water and went on. "We believe the journal entries are trying to explain elements of the armor we have yet to see. It mentions those sets of threes, references from the Bible. Three coverings of righteousness may refer to the Old Testament tent of meeting. Layers of goat's hair, ram skins dyed red, and hides of sea cows formed the roof of that tent. Perhaps these leathers were used to construct one of the pieces."

"Which would be quite delightful," Dr. Eloise broke in. "If our theory is correct—and we have already shared this with you—the armor may have come to us across millennia of time. Materials with spiritual significance would greatly increase its worth."

"I thought you said it wasn't worth anything," said Rob suspiciously.

"Not on the open market," Dr. Dale said quickly.

"Not monetarily," his wife added. "But what a find it would be to have a fragment of the most ancient house of Yahweh worship!"

Dr. Dale said, "We might be able to determine its geographic origins under an electron microscope; indigenous vegetation and pollen could be in the fibers."

The salads came.

"What about the three witnesses and judgments by fire?" Elijah asked. "And what about my name?"

"Very perplexing," said Dr. Dale, cutting his lettuce with a knife. "Three angel visitors came to Abraham before fire rained down on Sodom and Gomorrah. That's one idea, but there are other cases of three witnesses, such as Shadrach, Meshach, and Abednego in the fiery furnace."

Mrs. Elliston said, "The Lord is coming at the end, with chariots of whirlwinds, with fire and sword. That's in Isaiah."

Dr. Dale said, "Something to consider—the fiery final judgment."

I took all this in, thinking back to Elijah on the beach and at Camp Mudj, acting like some savage prince of fire. . . .

"How this all relates to the armor we can only guess. Hopefully a thorough review of the journals will clear things up."

Elijah gave his opinion. "Maybe at first Dowland thought of himself and his daughter and the baby as the only three righteous ones in town and that the rest should be wiped out by fire. Maybe that's why he burned down the church at the end. As a sign."

"Very good," said Dr. Dale. "Yes, thought-provoking."

"What about the threefold cord?" Elijah asked.

"The book of Ecclesiastes says that 'a cord of three strands is not quickly broken.' It means that though one may be overpowered alone, two or more together can defend themselves. Perhaps we'll find such a cord on one of the pieces of armor that symbolize this. Another possibility: King David once lined up his enemy prisoners and marked them off with lengths of cord. Every two lengths were put to death, the third length was allowed to live. This could explain why your name is given three times, Elijah."

Rob said, "That was my idea, that it was a hit list!"

Dr. Eloise flipped. "A superior deduction! It could be that he tried to do away with you twice and failed. The third time, he let you live."

Mrs. Elliston stopped eating, her fork in mid-air.

"We've been looking into it for weeks," Dr. Eloise said with a smile. "No stone unturned, all angles explored."

"Are you actually saying that that old man was trying to kill our kids over an old suit of armor? *Why?!*" Mrs. Elliston put her fork down. "Does Officer Taylor know this?"

Elijah said, "He knows Dowland set his dog on us."

Mrs. Elliston shot a look at Reece. "You didn't tell me that was a deliberate attack!"

"We don't know that it was, Mom. I didn't want to worry you."

Dr. Eloise said confidently, "Dowland is no longer a threat."

Reece squeezed her mom's arm. "It's okay."

Dr. Dale picked at his food. "Every true believer understands that the world can be dangerous, Mrs. Elliston."

Reece's mom stared off at the city lights, which were strung as far as you could see into the night, and said quietly, "That's true."

Dr. Eloise emphasized, "Perhaps one danger should be mentioned, as a warning to the five of you. It may be a tendency for anyone who owns the armor and understands its significance to be tempted by dreams of power and delusions of greatness. Apparently our Mr. Dowland became consumed. And it wasn't the first time, if the legends are true. . . ."

Dr. Dale summed up. "So let us stay on course of the wearer's purpose. In ancient days God often commanded his prophets to wear something strange or act out a drama as a visual of things to come."

"An omen," Elijah said quietly, turning his glass again.

"Yes," said Dr. Dale. "A truth about the future."

The waiter took our salad plates and brought the main course. The Stallards got a big charge out of treating us like dignitaries at the top of the town. I fought the urge to look out the window and tried to enjoy myself.

"Has anyone been thinking about the group dynamics question?" Dr. Dale brought up again.

I spoke up. "I don't know if this is what you're looking for, but here's my take on it: Rob's the brain and Reece is the mouth. . . ." She screwed up her face at me. "Mei is the eyes or hands because she draws."

"And Elijah?" Dr. Dale asked.

"He's the heart," I said.

We all got thoughtful.

"What about you?" Mrs. Elliston asked me.

"Me? I'm the ears . . . and the rhythm. These guys got no rhythm." I nodded toward Elijah and Rob. "You should have seen them at my grandparents' Pentecostal church. It was embarrassing."

We finished up dessert with two or three conversations going on at once around the table. Elijah went into his zone again, turning his glass around and around. "What's up with that?" I asked.

"This is the world. It's spinning."

"Yeah, and? . . ."

"Just think, the armor has been moving around the world for centuries and centuries. All kinds of people building onto it, wearing it, searching for it."

"That's pretty cool."

His eyes slid to me. "And soon it will be ours."

Something in his look sent chills down my spine.

# Chapter 27

DR. Dale paid the bill. Dr. Eloise patted her mouth with the linen napkin. "Now, what will it take to soften up our Mr. Theobald, so that you may have a look around his property?"

"A miracle," Reece said tiredly.

"Well, then," Dr. Eloise said, leading the way to the elevator, "that is what we shall have! Now who wants to see an authentic Babylonian terra-cotta demon head?"

"Woohoo," I said. "Hold me back."

We went by two taxis to an old museum in another part of town. I would have been pretty creeped if Mrs. Elliston hadn't been with us. The lab was in the basement and locked down like a prison with security systems and steel doors. No one else was around. We saw the artifact that had been packed in that wood coffin in the Stallards' office. It was an ugly dog-faced thing with broken teeth and empty eyes. Mei said it looked like the guardian statues at shrines in Japan.

"Why do you want this?" I asked.

Dr. Dale said, "He's not pretty, but he is important to understanding the culture in the seventh century B.C."

"Is it worth anything? How can you tell how old it is?" Rob asked. While he and the girls listened to a lecture about the shortcomings of carbon dating, Elijah and I checked out tables of bones and broken pottery. We kept our voices low.

I said, "The Stallards are cool in a weird way, but . . . did you notice that all the news articles on the bulletin board in their office were yellowed?"

"What's your point?" he asked.

"Maybe they're washed up, over-the-hill scientists, and the armor is a chance for them to stake some big claim."

Elijah didn't answer.

"My dad checked them out, but I don't know . . . look what happened to Dowland. He started out good. . . ."

Elijah picked up a bone, looked it over, and said, "We have to be careful."

The next morning we met back in the conference room to plan the retrieval from Theobald's yard.

"Now tell us again why you can't ask his permission?" Dr. Dale asked.

"He hates us," Rob said. "He'd shoot us."

They looked to Mrs. Elliston. She said, "I don't know. But until this man is cleared of all suspicion, I don't want them to have anything to do with him."

"What adjoins his property?" Dr. Dale asked.

"There are houses on both sides; and the railroad tracks curve around his property," Rob said.

"You're sure it's on his property?"

"Pretty sure," Elijah said. "It makes perfect sense that Dowland would have buried armor there. And there's a pile of fresh dirt under his rosebushes."

"Rosebushes," Dr. Eloise said, thinking out loud. "Sometimes they are used as border plants."

Dr. Dale said, "Exactly. It seems odd that a man would plant his treasure on his enemy's property. If only we had record of the property lines."

Rob perked up. "Land plats? Got 'em!"

He unzipped his backpack and presented the Stallards with a folder. They cooed over Rob, calling him "splendid" and "indispensable." He was twelve shades of red and loving every minute of it.

Elijah remembered seeing a rusty fence under the bush.

Dr. Dale announced, "All right. The burial spot was most likely on an easement for the railroad. Oh, I wish we weren't so decrepit and so over-scheduled. When's the best time to attempt retrieval?"

I said, "There's a lot of debris from the tornado around his house. It would be just our luck he'd bulldoze it all in a big pile on top of the site."

"So we need to hurry."

"Good morning!" Donovan walked in, wearing khakis and an oxford shirt. "I followed the smell of coffee."

Dr. Dale jumped up. "Donovan!" He shot his wife a knowing look and she shot him one back. "Donovan? Of course!"

"Good morning, dear," she said to him. "Yes, yes, have a cup and tell us what your schedule looks like for the next few days."

*He who walks righteously and speaks what is right . . .*
*this is the man who will dwell on the heights.*

—Isaiah 33:15, 16

# Chapter 28

※※※※※※※※※※※※※※※※※※※※※※※※※※※※※※※※※※※※※※※※

**MRS.** Elliston had a private talk with the Stallards and Donovan and didn't open up until we were almost home.

Elijah's mouth dropped open. "It's like Farr Island all over again! Combat simulation."

"Let me explain this to your parents," she said to us.

"My dad will okay it," I said.

"Mine too," said Elijah. When Rob didn't say anything, Elijah said, "And if it's okay with my dad, Rob will be able to do it too."

It was midnight on Monday, warm enough for T-shirts and shorts, but the four of us—we three guys and Donovan— were outfitted in black from head to toe. Instead of pluff mud, Rob brought some grease paint—it smelled a lot better than the mud. Even Donovan wore some. The parents weren't pumped about us creeping around the backside of town, but nobody could say no to Mrs. Elliston. Donovan would do the actual retrieval; we'd watch from the shadows.

He drove us into town and parked in the lonely lot behind the newspaper office. We'd already cased the site after school. It was deserted and dim with only one flickering security light.

"We'll follow the tracks to Theobald's house," Donovan said. "Elijah, you point me to the exact spot, then stay in the shadows unless I signal you otherwise. You are not to go onto any private property; and stay off the tracks. The whole operation should take no more than thirty minutes."

We opened the car doors, quiet as mice, clicked them shut, then slipped through the bushes. Scooting down the bank to the ravine, we followed the tracks without saying a word until we came in sight of Theobald's house, perched at the top of the bank. Elijah tapped Donovan's shoulder and pointed out the rosebushes. Donovan nodded and motioned for us to move into the underbrush. He took the shovel, crossed the tracks, and scrambled quietly up the bank.

Elijah had a talent for telling one shrub from another, even in the dark, so he'd worked out penlight signals with Donovan: one blink meant right, two left, and so on.

The Get Down training paid off. We sat in stone silence, patient, ready. We were on a mission.

Elijah grabbed my arm. "Train."

"What?" I couldn't hear a thing.

"Train," he whispered back. He nodded east.

I shook my head. But in a moment a faint, high-pitched squeal rose from the tracks. The hairs on my neck stood up.

"Brakes," he said, nodding east again. "Curve."

Sure enough, in a minute the distant *rick-a-tick* of a freight train reached my ears. I couldn't believe he'd heard it. "You're part bat."

"We're too close to the tracks," he said.

The bank above us was steep and rocky and loaded with shrubs. No place to go but to retreat toward the car.

Elijah pointed toward the train. "Under the bridge."

"Let's go," I said.

Rob led out. We'd only gone a few yards when a big light appeared ahead. He turned on us and whispered, "Can't make it. Go back! Go back!"

We backtracked to our old spot and tucked ourselves up under the scrub, a few feet above the tracks.

Elijah said, "We're safe, but it's going to feel close."

The freight train bore down on us like a monster with a gigantic white eye. The ground rumbled. The tracks screeched. I knew in my head we were safe, but every cell in my body shuddered. I was afraid of getting sucked under.

The train shot past with a burst of sound and a powerful whoosh of air. Then came a back draft from the other direction, like a wave and its undertow. The smell of hot grease mixed with the roar and rumble. We curled into trembling balls, covering our ears and eyes.

In a blast came screeching brakes, the rattle of freight car doors, the clack of metal on metal wheels and hitches and chains. It was as if all the disasters of the past few weeks had gotten on board. Something primal rose up in me. Safely drowned out, I yelled out in pure, exhilarated terror, screaming out all my pent-up feelings from the past weeks. Rob followed, then Elijah, all of us screaming bloody murder for a good two minutes. What a rush! Then the last car passed in a *whoosh*. The screeching tracks quieted. Our war cries died to a hush. I felt like I'd just come off a roller coaster. My soul felt as clean as day clean.

We sat up and watched the train recede west, a black hulk *clickety-clack*ing, getting smaller until it disappeared. "All body parts still attached?" I asked.

"Whoa," said Rob, excitedly. "That . . . was cool. I'm coming down here every night."

"No, you're not!" Elijah ordered.

"I can if I want."

"No, you can't. No more risky stuff."

"I'm not going to do anything stupid. Anyway, you won't know if I do or not."

"That's what you think," Elijah said.

I pictured Elijah creeping out at midnight, stashing himself in The Castle's big tree to hover over Rob like Metatron.

We swapped high fives and scooted down the bank to the tracks. We were dusting ourselves off when a shadow rushed up. "Got it!" It was Donovan holding a sack.

# Chapter 29

THE Stallards canceled their classes in Chicago. The next afternoon Elijah's dad ushered them into the meeting room at the lodge and left to run the camp. The Stallards gathered the five of us around the burlap sack on the table. Mei put on surgical gloves.

Dr. Eloise put up her hand. "Before we look at the artifact, I have something to tell you. On your good faith and trust in us, we will tell you about our names. Not our real names yet—we simply can't—but what our chosen names mean. They are made up," she turned to Elijah, "much like you made up your secret place of Telanoo. Now, you all know that one of the ancient names for God is *El*, don't you? It is the equivalent of the English word *God*. It's not his name actually, but what he is."

"El?" Elijah asked.

Dr. Dale said, "Yes. The *El* in your name means 'God.' I chose the name Day-El, as in the Day of El, the Day of the Lord."

"And *Eloise?*" Reece said.

"Code for the 'God of Israel,'" she answered. "El-o'-Is. We have used these aliases since we began working in The Window years ago. Our code names carry our purpose. We serve God to prepare believers for the Day of the Lord."

I felt guilty about my earlier suspicions.

Mei carefully took the breastplate out of the burlap sack.

Reece said, "We didn't find any words yet, or any clue to the 'piece by piece' mystery."

The Stallards frowned and fussed over it. They were impressed with the "simple nobility" of it. The breastplate was made of stiff patched leather, pierced with small, dark red brads: three at the neck, three at an angle near the center, one near each underarm, and two at the waist about six inches apart. A sort of collar or leather band went around the neck and ended in the front with metal knobs a few inches apart.

Looking for the word *righteousness*, Dr. Dale finally said in a frustrated voice, "It must be encrypted. Perhaps each piece will be increasingly more so. But if this is genuine, it will be there. Let's analyze materials."

We waited as they studied and touched and whispered, sometimes in another language.

"This leather is not like the leather on the belt," he said. "And the pieces are not all the same kind of leather. See the slight variations in color and texture? This piece looks something like calf leather, this as if from some wild beast. But it has been tanned and burnished to a similar finish. The leather lining is of a lesser grade. We'll need to test it," he said excitedly, smiling at his wife, "but it looks very, very old and in a marvelous state of preservation! These just might be the three coverings of righteousness!"

Reece touched it. "Do you think it's from the tabernacle, the first worship house?"

We took turns touching the hard, smooth leather. Mei ran her fingers along the seams. "How old would it be?"

Dr. Eloise said reverently, "If this is tabernacle material? Thousands of years old. We won't know until we take it to the lab and subject a fragment to heat. See, the older the leather, the lower the temperature at which its collagen fibers shrink. We will subject a small piece to gradually increasing heat. If it begins to shrink in low heat, we'll know it's old. We can date a piece of leather by noting the temperature at which it starts to shrink."

Dr. Dale ran his hand on the inside of the vest. "I suspect it is reinforced between the leather layers. The bronze knobs at the neck—look, Eloise, these are the ends of a metal piece, slipped into a hem around the neck."

She slowly worked out a flat metal collar. "My goodness! Why, it's a torc! Look, children, this is very similar to pieces worn by Celtic warriors from the time of the Roman Empire. It symbolized authority and warlike power. The knobs seem to be bronze, ornamented with red coral or enamel.

Dr. Dale turned the torc over in his hand. "Fascinating! We could have some Viking history here."

Rob perked up. "Viking! Hey, maybe the word is on the torc."

Dr. Dale turned a little flashlight on the flat metal ring.

"There are etchings, a kind of border of circular shapes—
Eloise, are those eyes? They are! See, children, the torc is
engraved with eyes all around."

"Like the wheels on the chariot of God," Dr. Eloise said
in awe. She held it up for us all to see.

"It's Quella time," I said. "What do I look for?"

"Ezekiel chapter one, starting at verse four," she said.

I punched in the reference and read, "'I looked, and I
saw a windstorm coming out of the north—an immense
cloud with flashing lightning and surrounded by brilliant
light. The center of the fire looked like glowing metal, and
in the fire was what looked like four living creatures.'"

"These are the creatures depicted on the belt," she
explained. "Go on to the passage about the wheels."

"'I saw a wheel on the ground beside each creature. . . .
They sparkled like chrysolite, and all four looked alike.
Each appeared to be made like a wheel intersecting a
wheel. . . . Their rims were high and awesome, and all four
rims were full of eyes all around.'"

She passed around the torc so we could touch the
etchings of eyes. "This is thrilling!" she said. "Like the
wheel—symbolic of God's qualities—his warriors will
always be on the move, always watchful. How fitting
that the armorer designed this into the breastplate
of righteousness, to remind the wearer that God sees
everything."

When we couldn't find the hidden word after another

half hour, we took a break; the Stallards wanted to see the camp. Reece went off by herself, and Elijah took us on the tour. The Stallards listened to him play tour guide while the rest of us talked about the trip to Farr Island, the tornado, the armor, our day in East Iffy, the meanings of names in *kanji*. On the way through Owl Woods, Rob popped open a little plastic case and showed off his sand dollar. We strolled along, listening to him tell the legend to Dr. Dale. Suddenly he came to a screeching halt. Mei was showing Dr. Eloise her Japanese-English dictionary when she stopped at the same time.

"Sand dollar!" Rob gasped.

"*Gi!*" Mei said. "It is *gi!*" She pointed at the dictionary.

"What are you talking about?" I asked.

"That's it!" said Rob. He took off for the lodge.

"It is *sei GI no mune ate!*" Mei took off right behind him.

We followed them back to the room, where they were hovering over the breastplate. Rob was about to jump out of his skin.

"Make sense, will you?" I said.

"The brads on the breastplate, they're the wounds of the cross!" He placed the sand dollar alongside the breastplate to show how the dark red brads lined up with the hand, feet, and side wounds.

Dr. Eloise said, "I see what you mean. Yes, yes, yes! And this row at the top replicates the crown of thorns. My word! The wounds of Jesus, the Lamb of God, his sacrifice covering our sin, embedded in the armor—why, it's simply elegant!"

Mei was so excited she stuttered. "And . . . and the . . . the lines . . . of sewing—"

"The seams?" Dr. Eloise asked.

"Yes, the seams! Look!" Mei pointed to a line in her dictionary. "This is the symbol for *righteousness*. It's in old style, but I'm sure. It is a Chinese character we use in our language." She traced the seams with her finger, like an artist using a brush.

Dr. Dale asked, "Chinese? It says *righteousness* in Chinese!?"

"And Japanese," she said. "Same letter, different pronouncing."

Dr. Dale pressed his fists on the table to steady himself. "Unbelievable! We never would have seen this, a Chinese character made from patchwork seams!" He nodded approval at Mei and Rob. "You are godsends!"

Reece came in, smiling. "Do you know yet?"

"We know!" Rob yelled. "We know!"

When the excitement died down, the professors asked Mei a ton of questions about her language and its symbolism.

"Japanese letters were originally word pictures, correct?" Dr. Dale asked.

"Yes," Mei said. "For example my name is Mei, but the letters mean 'living sprout.'"

"And what is the meaning behind this symbol, *gi?*"

Mei sucked air through her teeth. "Let me see . . ." She punched letters, then looked at the answer curiously. "The symbol for *sheep* is over the symbol for *me*. I don't know why that means 'righteousness.'"

The professors were bowled over. "The Lamb over me?" asked Dr. Dale. "An ancient Chinese letter holds the very picture of righteousness? Amazing!"

We ate lunch in a corner of the Camp Mudj cafeteria, our treasure back in humble burlap.

Dr. Dale couldn't keep a lid on. "If Rob and Mei had not seen those patterns in the artifact with their astute eyes, we might never have found it!"

I glanced at Reece. "You went off to pray about it, didn't you?"

The Stallards said they would keep our new treasure just long enough to test the age and nature of the materials.

"Well, okay . . . but I need it first," Rob said nervously. "Could you wait until tonight to take it? Or I could mail it to you, but I really need it . . . tonight."

"What's up?" I said.

He was red-faced and scared. "Just meet me at my house tonight."

# Chapter 30

ROB was as nervous as a turkey at Thanksgiving. He motioned us into his room and closed the door. "I'm going to put it on."

"Sure," Elijah said. "I wore the helmet all night once."

"And you brought the belt?" Rob asked.

Elijah handed it over. We helped him fit the breastplate over his head. We tightened it at the sides and back, and Elijah buckled the belt over it.

"So what's *righteousness* mean, exactly?" Rob asked, trembling.

"Being pure in heart," Reece said. "Doing what is right."

He fiddled with the belt. "Does that mean telling people what is right and wrong?"

"Sure. If people don't hear what's right and wrong, how will they know how to act?"

He stood in front of the mirror on his door, looking hard at himself for a long time. "People should do the right thing?" Rob asked, as if he needed to be convinced.

"Yeah," I said. "What's brewing?"

"Do what's right," Rob rehearsed. "You have to do what's right." He turned to the rest of us. "Will you go with me? I'm going to face my dad."

*No me digas!* I thought. *I don't believe it!*

The Wingates were showing the house to a potential buyer. We listened at the door until we heard only two voices. Rob went to the top step and took a deep breath.

"Wait," Reece said anxiously. "I want to have a ceremony, to bind us together to be a clan, like Elijah said. I really think we should."

I said, "Let's use that verse about the cords: 'Though one may be overpowered, two can defend themselves.'" I stuck out my fist. "'A cord of three strands is not quickly broken.'"

Reece put her hand in the circle and grabbed mine. "'A cord of three strands is not quickly broken.'"

Rob did the same, his voice shaking: "'A cord of three strands is not quickly broken.'"

"A cord of four strands is not quickly broken," Elijah said, reaching in.

"A cord of five strands is not quickly broken," Mei finished.

Reece smiled, satisfied. "That'll have to do. For now."

We followed Rob downstairs. His mom and dad were in the family room, looking over some papers.

"Mom?" said Rob, stiff as a board, shaking like a leaf. "Dad?"

They gave us a curious look.

"What is it, son?" Dorian Wingate said, acting all innocent. "What's that? A new costume?"

"It's not a costume, Dad. It's the breastplate of righteousness and the belt of truth." He gulped hard and went on. "What you're doing is wrong. It's wrong for me and it's wrong for mom and you too. You're not allowed to do wrong things." He hooked his thumb nervously over the belt. "That's the truth."

His dad smiled a sickening smile. "Now Robbie—"

Rage welled up in me, but I kept quiet.

"It's Rob now, Dad," he said. "My name's Rob. If you'd been around, you'd know that."

"Okay, Rob," he said, a little irritated. "I understand that you're upset—"

Rob's lip trembled. "I'm upset because this is wrong."

"This is an adult matter. . . ." He looked at the rest of us. "A *private, family* matter."

Tears streaked Rob's face, but he stood his ground. "No, it isn't. It's a kid matter; it's my family you're breaking up. Everybody knows, so it's not private either."

"I think your friends should leave so we can discuss this," his dad said.

Something took over Rob like I'd never seen. *You the man,* I said to him in my mind, *you the man!*

"They're with me and we're sticking together, and when things get tough we don't run off. Because we know something: A cord of five strands—" his voice cracked.

Elijah finished, "—is not quickly broken. God said so."

Rob's parents were speechless.

"So, Dad?" Rob shuddered under the strain. "Are you going to be a man?"

Dorian's smile went sour. "You kids need to leave now."

Reece stepped forward. "We're not leaving our friend. You can call our parents, Mr. Wingate, but I can't leave my friend, not while you're breaking his heart."

Mrs. Wingate's hand had gone to her mouth. She choked back a sob.

I stepped up next. "My mom and dad went through it, and they made it back. You can too, sir. My dad's my hero because he came back."

Elijah stepped forward. "Because of you, Uncle Dorian, Rob almost drowned in the ocean. But we rescued him. We were there then. We won't leave him now."

Both parents went slack-jawed.

Mei had stepped forward, terrified. "I am with my friends."

Rob hiccupped with sobs. "Be a man, Dad. Don't go."

We followed Rob to his room, helped him off with the two pieces of the armor of God. He packed his stuff while the rest of us hung around not saying much. Downstairs, the front door closed. Rob didn't skip a beat. He kept on packing and sniffling. Elijah said we should stay together, so I called Dad to pick us up and take us to Camp Mudj.

I sat by Rob in the back seat on the way. "Hey, Viking."

"What?"

"I couldn't have done that."

He didn't say anything.

"I mean it. I could never have done that. You've got guts. More guts than anybody I ever met. You the man."

# Chapter 31

I woke early, yanked on my jeans, and staggered out the front door of Elijah's house. Elijah was sitting on the porch, staring down at the lake. "Let's go," he said.

"Where?"

"Follow me."

He took off out the driveway toward the main road. I grabbed my board, threw it down, and caught up with him. By the time we reached the camp gate, I knew where he was headed.

We zipped through town and stopped in front of The Castle.

Ripped roof, boarded windows, downed limbs. Trashed.

"The raven's curse," I joked.

He just smiled.

"What?" I asked.

"What's missing?" he said.

"I don't know. Oh, Mrs. Bates. Bet the street sweeper got her."

"No." He was grinning wide.

"The limbs, the big ones anyway."

"Not that."

Then I got it. The sign—For Sale: Price Reduced—was gone. And there were two cars in the driveway.

"That," I said, "is seriously awesome."

"Signs," Elijah said with a grin. "Let's go tell Rob."

It was the last day of school. A more perfect day I'd never seen. Sunny breezes swept through open windows. Music floated through the hall. Outside little kids were going spastic on the school lawn. The world was one big party. I cleaned out my locker and gave a wink and a nod to Miranda Varner on my way out of homeroom. "See you round," I said.

"Hope so," she said back.

I caught up with Elijah in the hall. "Hey, Nature Boy."

"Hey," he said, and grinned.

The others soon fell in line. As we headed for the wide open door at the end of the hall, I had visions of us three guys dressed in fatigues, running wild in Telanoo, honing our war strategies. Rob's strength would be in planning, mapping out the area, knowing every nook. I'd have to keep that in mind. Elijah's game would focus on stealth and instinct. I'd need pointers from Dad if I was *ever* going to beat him.

I imagined the five of us hanging out around Elijah's infernos, or holed up in Rob's attic deciphering Dowland's mysterious journals. I'd already been thinking about where the guys and I could stage our own boo hag night of terror to scare the girls half to death.

The five of us burst out the front door of Magdeline

Independent. We stood there on the top step gazing over a green lawn and a flood of kids heading home. The sound of saws and hammers echoed around town—people still rebuilding from the storm.

The reject grave hadn't been exhumed; Old Pilgrim Church was a gaping hole. There was a town to mend first.

"Everybody want to go to my place for a powwow?" Elijah asked. "We've got some ancient shoes to find!"

"Where do we start?" Mei asked.

We all looked at Elijah. "We keep watching for signs, I guess."

Thinking back over our string of near disasters, I shuddered, "Signs!? Brace yourselves, my people."

Reece led the way down the steps. "The raven was a good sign, not a curse."

"Yeah, you're right," I agreed. "And all the other signs too."

The wave had thrown Rob back to shore; and the storm had cleared a path to the breastplate. What Dad had told Rob rang true for all of us: someone you can't see is helping you. We took off across the lawn.

Reece said, "It's like that one story about Elijah in the Bible, when God sent the wind, the earthquake, and the fire to show his power. But he was really in the still, small voice." She grinned at Rob, "Like a certain voice saying, 'Do the right thing.' That was the most awesome sign of all."

The new seniors jammed in cars and roared past, blaring

horns and yelling. Mei said excitedly, "Pass with care! We're freshmen now!"

A huge, winged shadow in the shape of a cross swooped over us. I thought it was a plane and looked up. It was the raven, cruising low. It caught our attention and banked off to the northeast, skimming the trees.

"Where's it going?" I asked.

Elijah stopped, got his bearings. "The cliffs," he said. "Council Cliffs State Park."

Rob said, "Hey, that's where I thought Dowland could have buried the—" he caught himself, looked around to be sure we weren't being followed, "the you-know-what . . . maybe."

"Let's do it!" I said. We headed down the street toward Camp Mudj.

I've been all over the world, imagined myself in all kinds of exotic places, and had more than my share of adventure. But on that restless first day of freedom, I couldn't have dreamed of a place that promised more mystery and intrigue than Magdeline, Ohio.

"Anyone feel like a hike?" Elijah asked, tossing a look in my direction.

"Whatever it takes, Creek."

The end

# THE PATH OF SHADOWS

SKID and Rob stretched out on the gazebo benches; I sat on the rail, propped my foot against the post, and looked out over Silver Lake. School was out—we were feeling free as birds, lazy as old dogs. We had the first three pieces of the armor of God in our possession: belt, breastplate, and shield. Three down, three to go. Summer spread out before us as wide and smooth as the lake. Casually I said, "Our last sign was the raven cruising toward Council Cliffs. Not much to go on . . . Dowland could've dug a hole anywhere along a path and buried the next piece."

"Those trails go for miles," said Rob thoughtfully, his arms folded, his eyes drifting drowsily around the gazebo rafters.

Skid shrugged. "We have all summer."

"I'm not worried," I said.

Looking for the armor of God was a big part of our lives now, even though we'd only started last fall. Reece had predicted that the quest would change my life, and she was right. Sure, I still had lots of regular duties at Camp Mudjokivi: pool cleaning, driving kids with disabilities around in the golf cart, campfire setup and cleanup, night hike preparation—whatever Dad needed. We always brought in college kids as summer staff, and it was my job to show them the ropes: rules, first aid, care of the equipment, identifying poisonous plants and bugs. I don't mean to sound like a jerk here, but sometimes I'm amazed at how much some college kids don't know about the real world.

Reece was baby-sitting all summer; Mei would be helping her mom with catering. Skid was hush-hush about his plans. Rob's parents got lots of insurance money from the tornado damage and went gangbusters on fixing up The Castle. They were always asking his advice about styles and colors so he'd feel included. We didn't hang around there much, still being kind of embarrassed about that face-off with Uncle Dorian over the almost-divorce. But Rob said they were working things out, and that was good. After his week "getting down to the Get Down" at Farr Island, the tornado nearly destroying his house, and then putting on the breastplate of righteousness and pulling his family back together, my cousin was a changed man.

On top of our separate duties, we had high school summer reading assignments. But for all of us, finding the armor of God was the number one priority.


"Bloocifer's loose! Elijah, HELP!!" My little twin sisters came barreling down the hill straight toward us, yelling and panicky. "Bloocifer's loose!"

I dropped down off my perch, my mind instantly in camp crisis mode. "Did you tell Dad?"

Skid sat up uneasily. "Who's Bloocifer?"

I said to the girls, "Okay. Get to the house and tell Mom. And tell Reece and Mei to stay put. Whatever you do, stay on the path. Now go!" They ran squealing toward home. I took off for the nature center, the guys following. I answered Skid as we ran. "He's a blue racer snake—fast, aggressive."

Mentally I swept the camp. A bunch of preschoolers were bug hunting in the wildflower meadow next to Frog Lagoon; middle schoolers milled around their cabins on the other hill. I could hear kids at the pool behind the lodge. *Blue racers like water,* I reminded myself.

"Bloocifer?" Skid asked worriedly. "You mean as in Lucifer?"

"Boo-Blue-Lucifer-Racer all in one. Rob thought up the name. Racers move up to eight miles an hour and have vicious bites. Bloocifer hates humans—especially me. I'm the one who caught him. Watch your step—he could be anywhere."

Rob's eyes were glued to the ground as we ran. "I've seen him pushing up the lid of his cage, trying to escape. He raises his head like a cobra and darts back and forth. He's a maniac! If you see a six-foot streak of light blue-green in the grass, run like the wind!"

# Ancient Truth

※※※※※※※※※※※※※※※※※※※※※※※※※※※※※※※※※※※※※※※※※※※※※※※※

*(page 7)* "He makes the clouds his chariot and rides on the wings of the wind.
He makes winds his messengers, flames of fire his servants."

**Psalm 104:3, 4**

*(page 12)* "Stand firm then, with the belt of truth buckled around your waist, with the breastplate of righteousness in place."

**Ephesians 6:14**

*(page 42)* "They were terrified and asked each other, 'Who is this? Even the wind and the waves obey him!'"

**Mark 4:41**

*(page 97)* "The LORD is slow to anger and great in power; the LORD will not leave the guilty unpunished.
His way is in the whirlwind and the storm, and clouds are the dust of his feet."

**Nahum 1:3**

*(page 159)* "See, the LORD is coming with fire, and his chariots are like a whirlwind;
he will bring down his anger with fury,
and his rebuke with flames of fire."

**Isaiah 66:15**

*(pages 160 and 178)* "Though one may be overpowered, two can defend themselves.
A cord of three strands is not quickly broken."

**Ecclesiastes 4:12**

*(page 166)* "He who walks righteously and speaks what is right,
who rejects gain from extortion and keeps his hand from accepting bribes,
who stops his ears against plots of murder and shuts his eyes against contemplating evil—
this is the man who will dwell on the heights, whose refuge will be the mountain fortress.
His bread will be supplied, and water will not fail him."

**Isaiah 33:15, 16**

# Creek Code

**Japanese**

*Ganbatte*—(gahm-bah-tay) Hang in there

*Kanji*—(kahn-jee) Chinese characters

*Sei gi no mune ate*—(say ghee no moo-neh ah-teh) Breastplate of righteousness

*Abunai*—(ah-boo-nah-ee) Dangerous

*Nihongo*—(nee-hone-go) Japanese language

*Sugoi*—(soo-goy) Wow

*Genki desu ka*—(ghen-kee des kah) How are you? Are you healthy?

*Konnichiwa*—(kohn-nee-chee-wa) Good day

*Gi*—(ghee) A kanji character meaning righteousness

**Spanish**

*Tranquilo, me hijo*—(tran-kee-lo may ee-ho) Take it easy, my son

*Comprende*—(kohm-pren-day) Do you understand?

*No entiendo*—(no en-tee-en-do) I don't understand

*No me digas*—(no may dee-gahs) You do not say to me (i.e., I don't believe it!)

**Hebrew**

*El*—a prehistoric, generic word for God. In the Bible it is often combined with other words. *El Shaddai* means "God Almighty"; *El-Elohe-Israel* means "God, the God of Israel."

# Mr. Skidmore's Eight Lessons

**Lesson One:** Sometimes you get stuck in a game where others don't play fair. War's not fair. Life's not fair.

**Lesson Two:** If you acquire some intelligence that will help you live a better life, then you win.

**Lesson Three:** If it hurts a little, that's okay, if you accomplish your goal.

**Lesson Four:** Use all your gifts and resources.

**Lesson Five:** Some fears are real, but most are created in your own mind.

**Lesson Six:** War has rules. But in the end war is not about rules or badges. Winning a just war is about love; good men fight only when they have to, to defend those they love.

**Lesson Seven:** When the enemy's on your heels, learn how to throw him.

**Lesson Eight:** Someone you can't see is helping you.

*Check out this other new series . . .*

## GAME ON!

*Stephen D. Smith with Lise Caldwell*

GAME ON! is a sports fiction series featuring young athletes who must overcome obstacles—on and off the field. The characters in these stories are neither the best athletes nor the underdogs. These are ordinary kids of today's culture—characters you'll identify with and be inspired by.

RED CARD
0-7847-1438-X

RIVALS ON THE WAVES
0-7847-1470-3

HIGH HURDLES
0-7847-1439-8

FOURTH AND LONG
0-7847-1471-1